John King

Bounty Hunter

By Robert J. Gossett

authorHOUSE®

AuthorHouse™
1663 Liberty Drive
Bloomington, IN 47403
www.authorhouse.com
Phone: 1-800-839-8640

Published by AuthorHouse 1/12/2012

ISBN: 978-1-4685-4038-3 (sc)
ISBN: 978-1-4685-4037-6 (hc)
ISBN: 978-1-4685-4036-9 (e)

Library of Congress Control Number: 2012900207

This book is dedicated to the late Shirley Jane Ranker who encouraged me to resume writing.

And to

Amy Slanchik, an excellent typist.

Sharon Slanchik, who overcame adversity to find time to edit this book.

John Slanchik for his superior computer skills.

Dennis Ray, for his unequalled knack for proofreading.

Tih Kobolson, for her excellent art work.

My sincere thanks to all of them.

Table of Contents

Chapter 1
College Days

John (sometimes called Jack) was a second-year law student at the University of Texas in Austin. He was an excellent student, getting straight A's. It was not because he studied that hard, but because he had a photographic memory. The night before a test he would read a textbook and refer to his memory to pass the test.

John was majoring in girls more than law. Almost six feet tall with an athletic build, girls were attracted to his dark complexion and blue eyes. The girls referred to him as a desirable bachelor who would be a fine catch. His male friends thought of him as a lucky guy. His jealous acquaintances called him a spoiled rich kid. They were right about the rich part, but in reality, it was his parents who were very rich.

His father, Jacob King, was a criminal defense attorney in Houston. His mother, Helen, was a tenured professor of English literature at the University of Houston. His father was Jewish and his mother, a Roman Catholic. Both children were encouraged to pick their own religion, so John chose neither. His younger sister, Sarah, a senior at Sam Houston High School, chose the Catholic religion, which greatly pleased their mother. John considered himself an agnostic. Their home in Houston was a large estate in River Oaks, which fit their positions in life.

The Kings also owned a 500-acre ranch west of Galveston. Their ranch manager, Juan Ortiz, handled everything about the ranch: the hiring and firing of the ranch hands; the cattle sales; the planting and cutting of coastal hay; and the management of ranch funds. As a reward for his twenty years of service, he was awarded a generous bonus of twenty percent of the ranch profits.

The Kings elected not to participate in Houston's society circle.

Instead they preferred to have quiet intimate dinners with friends, or an evening playing cards with neighbors or friends.

They led the good life and indulged their two children.

John rented an off-campus apartment in Austin where he entertained many of his girlfriends. Sarah lived at home and commuted to school in her own surrey, pulled by a very expensive sorrel gelding.

One Monday evening John was sharing a bottle of wine with Lola Bigelow. They were half-way through the bottle when there was a loud and rapid knock on the door. Lola ran into the bedroom to hide as John answered the door.

It was Sergeant Dick Smith from the campus police.

"John, I hate to break up your little party, but I had a telegram from Police Chief Mike Ward in Houston."

"What did it say?" John asked.

"It seems you have an emergency at home, and your family needs you at home right now," Smith reported.

"What's wrong?" John excitedly asked.

"Chief Ward will fill you in when he picks you up at the train tomorrow. I'll take you to the stage coach now and you can get to San Antonio in time to catch the morning train for home.

"And, oh yes, you can tell your little honey in the other room she can come out now," Smith told him.

"How did you know?" John asked.

Smith replied, "I am a cop, you know. One bottle of wine, two glasses, and the aroma of an expensive perfume were good clues."

John laughed and told Lola to come out and lock up when she left. He also asked her to tell Professor Moriarity he had to go home for awhile. Then he left with Smith to catch the stage for San Antonio, then the train to Houston.

It was late afternoon when Chief Ward picked him up at the depot. John knew Chief Ward from hunting trips his dad invited him on, and Chief Ward and his wife, Carol, had been at the King house numerous times for dinner and a game of cards. As John watched Chief Ward approach the depot he studied him carefully.

Mike Ward was a big man. He stood over six feet tall, had broad shoulders, a large chest, long arms, and big hands. His face with a warm smile and glasses looked friendly, but John guessed it could turn to stone in an instant, if necessary.

"Hello, Chief Ward," John greeted him.

"Hi John," came the reply. "I'm sorry, but I have some terrible news for you."

"I have worried all the way home—what is wrong?" John asked.

Ward replied, as he put his arm around John's shoulders, "I'm afraid your mother and dad have been murdered."

"Oh, shit, what happened?" John asked, struggling while trying to fight back tears.

Ward continued, "Well, it appears to me someone broke in trying to rob them, and it turned bad from there."

"What about my sister?" John asked.

"Well, she is still alive but someone tried to strangle her, and she was repeatedly raped," Ward told him.

"Who did it?" John wanted to know.

Ward told him, "That's what we are trying to find out now. The cook and maid found them yesterday morning and notified me right away. I was at your house by eight o'clock and checked the entire house, but whoever did it was gone."

"How were they killed?" John asked.

Chief Ward told John, "You might want to sit down; your knees look a little wobbly."

John said, "Just tell me, I'm OK."

"Well, your dad was stabbed and shot. Your mother was raped and strangled," Ward revealed.

"Are they still at home?" John wanted to know.

"No, son, I had the undertaker pick up your parents, and your sister is in St. Anne's Hospital. Want me to take you there now?"

"Yes, please."

"OK, but remember, she is in pretty bad shape. They also beat her on the head, and the doctor told me she has a bad concussion. I tried to question her, but she drifts in and out of consciousness, and she is not lucid when she is awake," Chief Ward warned John.

Ward drove John to the hospital and then waited in the visitor's lounge so John could visit Sarah by himself.

Sarah was asleep when John reached her bedside. As he kissed her and hugged her she stirred but did not wake up.

He whispered in her ear, "Sarah, oh Sarah, I am so sorry this happened to you. I love you and I will be back when you are awake." Still no response.

Then he met Chief Ward in the visitor's lounge. "Did you talk to her?" Ward asked him.

"No sir, I couldn't get her to wake up, but I tried to tell her I would be back when she wakes up," John replied.

"John, I'm afraid you are going to have to accept a lot of responsibility from here on. I talked to your Dad's junior partner, David Samuels, and he will help you with everything he can," Chief Ward told him.

"The main thing is I want those sons of bitches that did this caught and hanged, even if I have to do it myself," John warned.

"Now, John, take it easy. We'll catch them, but as a law student you should know to let the law handle this," Ward said.

"Who all is working the case?" John asked.

"We all are. Every man in the department is working on it, and I am leading the investigation myself, so we will get them," Chief Ward told him.

"I guess I want to go home now," John said, still in a state of shock and confusion.

"OK, I'll take you. I asked the two servants to clean up the house a little bit because we had already released it, so it should be OK for you to stay there if you want to," Chief Ward said.

"I do want to. I will be OK," John said.

Lisa, the cook, and Maria, the maid, met him at the door, gave him a hug and told him how sorry they were.

John asked them to stay on and he would pay them for at least as long as he kept the house. They agreed to do so. John wandered aimlessly from room to room. In his parents' room he saw that the girls had stripped his parents' bed, but the mattress was still stained with blood on both sides.

His sister's bed had also been stripped, but it too had blood stains from top to bottom on the mattress. Every drawer in both rooms had been removed and the contents, thrown on the floor. All books from the book cases were also scattered on the floor. When he entered his father's study he saw that it, too, had been ransacked. The picture of his parents' wedding had been removed, and a wall safe behind it had been hammered open and emptied. The gun case had also been emptied.

Brokenhearted, John walked to his room and collapsed on his bed, sobbing with despair.

The next morning, his stomach growling with hunger, John sat down to enjoy the breakfast Lisa had waiting for him. The bacon, eggs, grits, and biscuits filled him up quickly and the coffee hit the spot.

As he was finishing his third cup of coffee, David Samuels arrived and sat with him to have coffee.

"John, I know this is awfully soon, but if you can come by the office this morning, I have a lot of papers for you to sign. There is also a safe at the office only your dad had the combination to. If you like I will have a bonded locksmith open it while you are present," David told him.

"Thanks, David, I can do that, but first I need to go by the hospital and see Sarah," John replied.

Finishing his coffee, David headed for the door and said as he left, "See you in a couple of hours."

John went to the carriage house and saddled his dad's favorite horse, a black stallion he called Diablo.

It was a short ride to the hospital, and he first spoke to Sister Hortense.

"How is Sarah this morning, Sister?"

She reported, "Not much change, I'm afraid."

Disappointed but undaunted, John went to Sarah's room. He was determined to learn from her who the assailants were.

He spoke to her, "Sarah, sweet Sarah, are you awake?"

There was no response so he said, "Sarah if you can hear me, give me some kind of signal."

Again, there was no response, so John left, telling Sister Hortense he would return tomorrow.

He mounted Diablo and rode to his dad's law office. The sign still read,

Jacob King—Attorney at Law
Specializing in Criminal Defenses

David and a locksmith were waiting for him, and they watched as the safe was opened. David paid the locksmith and he left.

"Do you mind if I watch as you empty out the safe?" David asked.

"Of course not," John replied, and he began to remove the safe's contents and pile it on his dad's old desk.

Jacob King had been a very methodical man and had carefully cataloged the contents. One envelope was marked stocks and bonds. It contained bonds from Harris County, bonds from City of Houston, and bonds from the State of Texas.

It also contained shares of stock in Wells Fargo Stage Lines; Houston State Bank; Bigelow Oil Exploration and Refining; Kansas City Southern Railroad; and Shiner Brewing Co.

David whistled and said, "Wow, I'd guess you are looking at close to a million dollars there."

Then John took out an envelope marked "Cash." It was heavy because it contained both U.S. cash in large bills and gold coins. A quick estimate put this envelope worth about $20,000.

John commented, "This is probably what the bastards were looking for at home."

David agreed, "Probably."

The last envelope was marked "Wills."

It contained both wills from Jacob and Helen. They were both simple "Mom and Dad" wills leaving everything to each other, or split between John and Sarah equally.

John put the cash into a small valise, pocketed the gun list to take to Chief Ward, handed the wills to David to process for him, then reloaded the balance of envelopes back into the safe. He pocketed the combination the locksmith gave him and turned his attention to the papers David had prepared for him.

He signed the papers transferring all of his mother and dad's bank accounts to him, a power of attorney to take control of all of his parents' property, and a power of attorney to act in Sarah's behalf where she was incapacitated.

Then he thanked David and told him he would expect a bill for the services he had performed for him and his family.

David said, "We'll talk about that later. You know, I would like to buy your dad's practice, but all that can wait until after the funeral."

John agreed and left for Chief Ward's office to deliver the gun list.

Mike said to John, "I know your father was thorough, but just look at this list."

They read down the list together:

1 WH Tisdall and Son double-barrel shotgun
12 Gauge 28" Barrels S/N 734
1 WH Tisdall & Son double-barrel shotgun
12 Gauge 30" barrels S/N 811

1 cased-set English Flintlock dueling pistols
Caliber 36 hand-made no S/N

Chief Ward commented, "This will be a huge help in breaking this case. If we find the guns, we'll find the killers, and this list will be great evidence at the trial."

"Hope you find them soon," John said then left for the funeral home. He met with Mr. O'Dell.

O'Dell commented, "If you want a double funeral, it could be a little tricky with your father a Jew and your mother a Catholic."

"Well, they would have wanted a joint funeral, so you work it out, and I'll help you if I can," John said.

Exhausted from the day's activity, he rode home, found his dad's stash of brandy, and poured himself a large glass.

The girls had the day off, so John made himself an egg sandwich, drank a glass of milk, and went to bed.

Chapter 2
Instant Manhood for John

John woke up the next morning, and as was his habit he remained in bed and thought about what he had to do that day. He tried doing this at night before he went to sleep, but when he did he had trouble sleeping.

John thought, *Today I have to go see Sarah at the hospital, visit Chief Ward, and then attend my parents' funeral. I sure miss the life I had at school. Those were the good times, and they are gone forever.*

The funeral was unusual but done in very good taste. The caskets were placed side by side in the front of a viewing room at the funeral home.

Rabbi Amoskowitz stood in front of his father's casket, and father O'Malley stood in front of his mother's. Each took his turn saying prayers over the two caskets.

It was not generally known but the Rabbi and the priest belonged to the same poker club. Together with other clerics they met monthly to play penny ante poker and poke fun at each other's religion. They always stopped short of blasphemy.

When the Rabbi and priest finished their prayers, the funeral director gave a short speech about the decedent's accomplishments.

When the funeral ended, the Rabbi accompanied Jacob's casket to the Jewish cemetery. The priest went with Helen's casket to the Catholic cemetery.

John stayed at the funeral home to converse with his parents' friends and neighbors. He was asked several times, "Do you know who did this?"

"No, but Chief Ward is personally looking into the case, and I feel sure he will catch them," John told them.

The next morning John went to see Sarah at the hospital. Sister Hortense met him at the door excitedly saying, "John please rush in to see your sister! She is awake, but I don't know for how long."

John rushed to Sarah's bedside, kissed her on the forehead and asked her, "How do you feel?"

"Dizzy," she replied.

"Sarah, try and remember, do you remember who did this to you?" John asked.

Sarah weakly replied, "I think I saw four men."

"Did you know them?" he asked.

"No, but one was black, one was a Mexican, and two were white," she told him.

Then she sank back into unconsciousness.

John was anxious to share this information with Chief Ward, so he hurried toward the door. Sister Hortense stopped him and asked him for a minute to talk to him.

"Sister, I'm in a big rush to see Chief Ward right now. Can it wait until I come in the morning?" he asked.

"I suppose so," the Sister said.

"Then, see you in the morning," he told her and hurried to the police station.

He saw Chief Ward sitting at his desk so he rushed to him, saying, and "Chief, Sarah woke up long enough to tell me who her attackers were!"

"Did she know them?" Mike asked.

"No, but she did say one was black, one was a Mexican, and two were white."

Mike deflated him a little by saying, "Well, that's a start, but not a hell of a lot to go on."

"Is it OK if I look through your wanted posters to see if I can find anyone who might fit the bill?" John asked.

"Sure, here they are," Mike said and handed him a stack of posters several inches high.

John spent the entire afternoon looking through the posters. He found a lot of pictures of Mexicans, several pictures of blacks, and lots of white men. He was discouraged that there were so many, but he was also amazed that so many men had such large bounties on their heads. He told Chief Ward he found nothing, said *"Adios,"* and went home.

He had missed lunch so he was hungry. Lisa had pork chops, applesauce, and beans ready for him. Again he enjoyed a glass of brandy and retired early.

Again the next morning he ate an early breakfast then headed for the hospital. He was anxious to continue his conversation with Sister Hortense.

As he walked into Sister Hortense's office, she greeted him, "John, I am so glad you came while Dr. Seidman is still here. He is one of the best experts on head injuries, traumas, and comas."

"Hello," they both said as John shook his hand.

Sister Hortense continued, "Dr. Seidman has just finished examining your sister, and I'll let him give you his opinion."

Dr. Seidman said, "John, I'm afraid your sister's prognosis is not good. She has one of the worst head injuries I have ever seen, and her chances of regaining a productive life are slim to none."

John winced, and Sister Hortense patted his arm.

"What does that really mean, Doctor?" John asked.

"I'm afraid it means we will not be able to do much more for her here," the doctor replied.

Sister Hortense interrupted, "John, we both think you should consider moving her to a private facility where she can get constant care. The Carmelite nuns have one here in town, called Saint Agnes."

"That is a good facility," Dr. Seidman commented. "I do visit patients there. It is a lot less expensive than here, and frankly, she will be better cared for."

"Where is it?" John asked.

"Not far from your home. And if you like I can give you directions and a letter of introduction to Sister Ruth," Sister Hortense told him.

"That would be nice of you. I'll go see it this afternoon," John said.

John had been thinking all morning about the wanted posters he saw earlier. His photographic memory recalled the two black men in the pile of posters. The first one, Ricky Johnson, was wanted for armed robbery of a bank. The second one he looked at featured Willie Washington, who was wanted for burglary, rape, and murder. John decided he would be a good suspect to start with.

On his way to St. Agnes, he stopped by his dad's old office to visit with David Samuels.

"Hello, John," David greeted him.

"Hello, David. I need your help," John said.

"I'll do whatever you ask, but John, if you don't mind, I'd like to tell you how much you have changed," David commented.

"How is that?" John asked.

David replied, "You have completely changed. You used to be a happy-go-lucky guy, and now you are a serious man who gives orders very easily."

"I've had to change, and in a hell of a hurry. I have huge responsibilities, the most important being discovering who killed my parents," John answered him.

"I understand, John, but how can I be of assistance?"

"I need you to set up a trust fund, the Jacob and Helen King Memorial Fund. I am to be the head administrator and you are to be the secretary who issues checks. I won't have to co-sign every check, only ones over $1,000. I know you won't cheat me because the consequences would be too severe for you to handle."

"Sure, I will get busy on that right away," David replied, a little shocked by the implied threat.

Without the usual amenities, John left for St. Agnes following the very detailed map Sister Hortense gave to him. When he arrived at St. Agnes and met Sister Ruth, he was taken aback by her looks. She was the complete opposite of Sister Hortense.

Sister Hortense was past middle age, tall, plump, and an always sober-faced.

Sister Ruth was petite, young, with a beautiful face she tried to disguise with horn-rimmed glasses. John guessed she had a beautiful figure judging from her large breasts that she tried to conceal under a loose fitting habit. John studied her for a minute. Then he thought to himself, *I wonder what she would look like naked.*

Then his mind told him, *"John, you should be ashamed of yourself for mentally undressing a nun."*

John introduced himself and Sister Ruth said, "Oh, yes, Mr. King, Sister Hortense told me about you and your sister. What a terrible thing to happen to both of you."

Then Sister Ruth took him on a tour of the facility. John was impressed with the cleanliness and order he found there.

"Are you Catholic?" Sister Ruth asked.

"No, but my sister is," John replied.

He didn't like the fact that one wing of the hospital was reserved for insane people, or "mentally deficient," as Sister Ruth called them.

He mentioned this to Sister Ruth, but was reassured that they were completely isolated from the rest of the hospital. Sister Ruth explained to him the hospital charged $5.00 per day, plus the cost of any medicines they had to administer.

John agreed to the price and told Sister Ruth they would receive a check monthly from the Jacob and Helen King Memorial Fund.

Sister Ruth told him she would arrange to have Sarah transferred the day after tomorrow. John said good-bye and left for the police station.

Chief Ward met him and said, "John before you ask, we don't have any new developments in the case, but we are all working our asses off on it."

John told him, "Mike, I have been thinking all day about one of the wanted posters."

"Which one?" Mike asked him.

"That Willie Washington. His poster says he is wanted in Nacogdoches for burglary, rape, and murder. Can you find out and more about him?" John asked.

Mike Ward told him, "Sure I can. I'll get a wire off today to Nacogdoches. Check back with me in a couple of days, and I'll share the information with you."

John told Mike, "Thanks, Mike. You are a good friend," and left for home tired from the day's activities.

A large glass of brandy made his dinner taste even better. The beef brisket, potato salad, and baked beans' aroma reminded him he had missed lunch, but he made up for it by eating twice as much for dinner.

The next day John did not visit Sarah as he thought they would be moving her to St. Agnes. Instead he rode to his dad's favorite gunsmith, Oscar Tyler.

As he entered the store Oscar greeted him, "John, it is so good to see you. I am so sorry about what happened to your family."

"Thank you, Oscar. I think I would like your help selecting some weapons," John replied.

"Glad to help you any way I can," Oscar said.

"Well, I figure on hunting for the killers, and I'll need a full arsenal of weapons to take with me," John explained.

"What will you need?" Oscar asked him.

"I have thought a lot about it, and I'll need a Colt Peacemaker in .45 caliber with a 4-inch barrel; a Smith and Wesson top break revolver in .44 caliber with a six-inch barrel; a Remington double-barrel Derringer in .41 caliber; a Colt Lightening in .38 caliber; a Sharps carbine in 45/70 caliber; and a Winchester rifle in .44/40 caliber."

"And a bowie knife," Oscar told him.

"That's some arsenal, but I think I have all of them in stock. How about leather for them?"

Yes, I'll need a quick draw holster for the Colt, a cross-draw holster for the Lightning; a shoulder holster for the top break, and a pocket in the cartridge belt under the quick draw holster for the Derringer; and scabbards for the two rifles and knife. And I want all of them in black with a silver crown inlaid in them," John instructed them.

"That's a tall order. I have a leather worker I use sometimes. He is expensive and slow but he does fine work. I think I can have it all ready in three or four days," Oscar told him.

"See you then," John said and left for the police station.

Chief Ward told him, "I have a wire from Joe Jones, police chief in Nacogdoches. Keep it if you wish," John scanned the wire, which read,

> To Mike Ward—Chief of Police, Houston, Texas. Willie Washington is wanted here for robbing and killing Mr. and Mrs. Bob Barrett, President of Citizen's Bank. Missing was cash, guns, jewelry, and silver. Believe he acted alone. No sign of him in over a year. We believe he fled to Arkansas. Good luck in finding him. Reward is $2,000 dead or alive.   —Signed, Chief Jones

First John quickly scanned the wire, then reread it carefully and folded it and put it in his shirt pocket.

Saying "Thanks" and *"Adios"* to Chief Ward, John set out for St. Agnes to visit Sarah. When he arrived he looked up Sister Ruth, who led him to Sarah's room.

"Did she wake up at all?" John asked.

"I'm afraid not," she answered.

John went in to her room, kissed her on the forehead, but no response at all.

"Sister, do you think she will ever wake up again?" John asked her.

"Only God knows, but if she does we will notify you instantly," Sister Ruth replied.

"Thank you, Sister," John answered, and left for home and another of Lisa's delicious meals.

After dinner over coffee, John sat down with Lisa and Maria and told them, "In a few days I will be leaving on a long trip. I might be gone three weeks or longer. Maria, I would appreciate it if you could pack me a valise with some clothes and fix me a bed roll with a sleeping pad, and wrap it in my poncho. And Lisa, please fry me up some food I can take along. I will be taking a pack mule, but pack it light. I hope you will both stay on here. I'll add some money to the household money and include your wages in it."

"Where are you going?" they asked in unison.

"Well, hopefully I will be on the trail of one of my family's killers. I'm convinced if I catch him, he will tell me who the rest of the killers are."

"Oh, John, do be careful," Maria said.

"Yes, come home to us," Lisa added.

Chapter 3
The Chase Begins

"Don't worry, I will be careful, and I will be back," he promised. In a few days his weapons were ready. John left to pick them up. They were all laid out on a table waiting for him. Oscar quoted the price, and John paid him. Oscar said, "Because you didn't haggle over the price, I am going to throw in a box of ammo for each of the guns, and a saddle bag to hold all of it. Your dad always haggled over the price, and he usually got me down in price. He was a good haggler."

John laughed as he said, "He loved to haggle. Just put all of these in a feed sack, I'll put them on later."

John then rode to St. Agnes to see Sarah. There was no change in her condition. He explained to Sister Ruth, "I will be out of town for several weeks, so if there is any change, please tell Chief Ward. He will know how to get in touch with me."

Then he went to see Mike Ward and told him he was leaving town for a spell but would wire him of his progress.

Mike Ward's face turned stone cold as he told John, "You be careful, and don't do anything illegal or I'll have to arrest you."

"Don't worry, Mike, I'll stay within the law."

They shook hands and John left to visit David Samuels.

He explained to David he had a lead on one his parent's killers and was going to East Texas to check on him. He instructed David to pay St. Agnes once a month, and to check on Lisa and Maria once in a while to make sure they were OK.

David agreed, and then John, satisfied he had made arrangements for his departure, rode home for dinner and to examine his purchase.

That evening after dinner he went to his room to examine his purchase. He carefully loaded his firearms and put the balance of ammunition in his saddle bags.

The next morning John was up early, had a light breakfast, and told Lisa and Maria "Good-bye." Both of them hugged him and instructed him to be careful.

After three hard days of riding he arrived in Nacogdoches and went directly to the police station.

Chief Joe Jones met him at the door. Chief Jones had red hair and red bushy eyebrows. He was short in stature but had a muscular build. His face was highly suntanned, and that along with deep squint lines betrayed his spending a lot of time in the sun. He wore a white western shirt, blue jeans, and a Colt Peacemaker in a tied-down holster.

Chief Jones said, "You must be John King. I had a wire from Chief Ward to expect you. What can I do for you?"

John told him, "I am looking for Willie Washington. He is wanted for questioning in the murder of my parents and the rape of my sister."

"Well, he shouldn't be hard to find. He is six feet, six inches tall, big-boned, with huge hands and feet. I originally thought he fled to Arkansas, but since then he has been sighted in Lufkin," Chief Jones said.

"Can you tell me about him?" John asked.

"Well, we want to talk to him about the murder of a bank president and the rape and murder of his wife. Personally, I doubt he would rape or murder. He is just a thief. I think he had a partner who did the rape and murders."

"Has he been in trouble before?" John wanted to know.

"Yeah, but only for being drunk and petty theft. We always tried to cut him some slack because of his childhood. He was born into slavery and worked in the fields since he was 16 years old. I would describe him as a gentle giant and a little dim-witted. He told me once that the overseer used to beat his mother for trying to protect him. One of my officers described him as not having a full cartridge belt," the chief explained.

"What makes you think he was in on the banker's murder?" John asked.

"We had reports he was at the flea market trying to sell silver candle sticks and a silver tea set that were missing from the murder scene," Chief Jones reported.

"Is he dangerous?" John asked.

"I don't think so. In fact, I would already have him in custody if we weren't so busy chasing hijackers who were stealing shipments of oil headed to our refinery here in town. They robbed two straight loads of oil from Bigelow Oil in Dallas, and the last one they robbed they also killed the driver, who was a woman. That got the mayor on my ass because the governor is on his, so we have to catch these guys," Chief Jones reported.

"I can understand that," John agreed.

"Oh, yes, one more thing; Willie likes to drink Shiner beer. And he chews Mail Pouch tobacco," John added.

"Well then, I think I'll just ride up to Lufkin in the morning and look around," John told the chief.

Chapter 4
Willie Washington

John rode toward Lufkin, stopping in every small town or wide place in the road that as yet was not a town.

He was amazed there were so many black people in East Texas. One local finally explained that many freed slaves did not understand what being free meant since they had never before known freedom. If they had been slaves under a benevolent master they stayed on and worked for wages, at the same farm where they had been slaves. Those who had masters or overseers who beat them moved on to other places, willing to face the dangers of the unknown. That was the case with Willie Washington. John had to feel a certain amount of sympathy for him.

For three weeks John wandered from place to place. When he found a saloon he would order a Shiner beer. If the bartender said they had none, John would make some excuse and leave. He figured Willie would not hang out in a place that did not serve his favorite beer. His next stop would be a diner where he would order a cup of coffee and inquire if anyone knew Willie. Finally after two weeks of failure and frustration he arrived in Lufkin. After spending the night in a very dirty rooming house, he rode to a diner to have a much-needed breakfast.

The waitress was a cute girl named Linda. She was not a young girl anymore but well preserved with a young-looking face. John guessed she was in her thirties, and she wore no wedding ring.

He decided to eat there and stay and talk to Linda.

She said, "Why all the crowns on everything?"

"That's because I am a King--John King," he replied.

"That's clever," she answered. "You're not from around here, are you?"

"No, I'm from Houston, looking for someone," he answered her.

"Who might that be?" she asked.

"His name is Willie Washington. Do you know him?"

"I might," she teasingly answered.

"What do you mean, you might?" John asked her.

"That depends on who you are and what you want with him," she said.

John lied, "He loaned a friend of mine some money and I'm here to pay him back."

"Well, in that case, he is a dishwasher here, but he doesn't come to work until five this afternoon."

John thought, *I can't believe I finally got lucky.*

Then he said, "I'll be back this afternoon for dinner. Will you still be working?"

"Sure. I don't get off until eight, so I'll see you this afternoon," Linda told him

"Good, see you then," John answered, and then went to find a place he could wait and watch the front of the diner.

Luckily there was a saloon across the street from the diner. John went in, ordered a beer, and sat at a table by the window where he could watch the front of the diner.

Time passed slowly, and he kept checking his pocket watch. After slowly sipping three beers he spotted a very large black man walking towards the diner. It was four-thirty.

John walked casually across the street as if he intended to enter the diner, then he intercepted Willie. He allowed him to pass, then drew his Colt and pushed it against Willie's back.

"Willie, you are under arrest. Don't resist or try to escape or I'll kill you," John warned him.

Willie was very surprised and said, "Don't shoot me Mistah! I ain't got no gun, and I ain't goin' to fight."

John put manacles on Willie's wrists and felt Willie's pockets. There were no weapons.

"How come you're restin' me, and who might you be?" Willie asked.

Being careful not to impersonate a police officer, John answered, "I'm John King from Houston. Does the name King mean anything to you?"

"Nevah heard of you," Willie answered.

"Well I'm trying to find the men who murdered my parents and raped my sister and turned her into a vegetable."

Willie answered, "I nevah killed or raped nobody."

"I almost believe you, so we'll let the law sort it out," John said.

Seeing the commotion, Linda came out of the diner and screamed, "John, what in the hell are you doing to my friend Willie?"

"Just taking him back to Nacogdoches to answer some questions," John replied.

"Miss Carol, he thinks I keeled somebody," Willie blurted out.

Carol said, "John, you son of a bitch--you lied to me."

"Sorry, but I had to find Willie," John said.

Carol blurted out, "Poor Willie would never hurt anyone. He is a harmless, gentle man who would never hurt a fly."

"After seeing him, I almost believe you, but he still needs to answer some questions back in Nacogdoches," John explained.

Still upset, Carol spun around abruptly and went back into the diner.

During the ride back to Nacogdoches they talked a lot. Willie admitted he had been at the King house during the attack but hurt no one. He identified a man called Indian Bob, and two brothers called Caleb and Carl Keegan as the rapists and killers. He claimed he only robbed while the violence went on. John thought to himself, *I actually believe him. He doesn't seem the type who would hurt anyone.* Under other circumstances they might have been friends.

John handed over Willie and was given a hearty handshake and a voucher for $2,000 from the city of Nacogdoches. He endorsed the voucher and handed it back to the sheriff, saying, "After spending a lot of time with Willie, I don't think he is capable of killing anyone. Please use this money to hire him a good lawyer, and when he is free, give him money to get back to Lufkin. He has a good friend there."

He was also handed a telegram from Chief Ward telling him to come home immediately. There was another emergency. John's adrenaline kicked in, and he pushed Diablo and the pack mule to the limit and reached home in two days. He went instantly to police headquarters and met with Chief Ward.

Mike told him, "Sit down, John, so I can give you some terrible news."

"Did something happen to Sarah?" he asked.

"No, she is fine, but about to be thrown out of St. Agnes," Mike told him.

"How can that be? Isn't Samuels sending them a check every month?"

"John, that's how I first learned that something was amiss. Sister Ruth and some guy called Murnahan came here to file a complaint against you for non-payment of a hospital bill. I know you told me Samuels would pay them monthly. Anyway, I went to see Samuels about it, but the only thing in the office was an empty safe."

"But where is Samuels?" John asked.

"That's just it. Samuels is gone, and so is everything you owned. Your house, the office, and all of the furnishings were sold, and the money paid to Samuels," Mike explained.

"Holy shit," John blurted out.

"Do you know what was in the safe?" Mike asked.

"I sure as hell do. There was over a million dollars worth of stocks and bonds, and deeds to the office building and my home," John said.

"That dirty bastard Samuels. I will kill that son of a bitch," John angrily commented.

"First things first. Let's start out by going to St. Agnes and square things there. I had to guarantee to pay her bill so Sarah wouldn't end up in a county charity hospital," Mike said.

"Let's go there now," John said.

"OK, but first take off those damned black chaps. Dressed the way you are you look like something that just stepped out of somebody's worst nightmare," Mike told him.

"How about my bank accounts?" John asked.

"That money is still yours. Apparently Samuels tried to get it, but the bank refused to change it over," Mike explained.

"How about the ranch?" John asked.

"Oh hell, I forgot about the ranch. After St. Agnes we'll go to the land office and check on it," Mike suggested.

During the ride to St. Agnes John said, "At least we'll get to see that pretty sister Ruth."

"Oh, you noticed that too," Mike said.

At the hospital they met with Sister Ruth who asked Murnahan to join them in her office.

Sister Agnes spoke first. "Young man, you should thank Chief Ward. Without his payment guarantee, we would have had no choice but to move your sister to the county charity hospital. We have had several cases where people have dropped off relatives here, just to get rid of them, and then just disappeared."

"How much is the bill now?" John asked him.

Murnahan spoke up, "Well, let's see now, $35.00 a week times seven weeks; that comes to $245.00."

"John took out a pile of money from his money belt and handed it to Murnahan saying, "Here is $500.00. Just post the rest to future bills, and I'll come back later with more."

"Thank you," Murnahan said, and he gave John a receipt.

Then John asked Sister Ruth, "How is my sister? Any change?"

"I'm sorry to say there has been no change. We have to force feed her, and even then there is no response," Sister Ruth explained.

John wanted to check on Sarah for himself. He bent over; he kissed her on the forehead and whispered in her ear, "Sarah, I am so sorry this happened to you. I promise you I will get everyone responsible. I will either kill them or make sure they are arrested and brought to trial."

Then he kissed her again and patted her hand. Then John returned to Sister Ruth's office where Mike had waited so he could spend time alone with his sister.

John reported there had been no change. He was unable to get any response from her.

"I promised her I would make every one of her attackers pay with their lives."

Sister Ruth winced. Saying their goodbyes, Mike and John took their leave.

"Mike, I will never be able to repay you for what you did for me."

"Just take me on a hunting trip sometime at the ranch--that is, if you still have a ranch," Mike told him.

They felt a little better after learning the ranch was still in the King family name.

"I guess the bastard forgot about the ranch," Chief Ward said.

"He probably wasn't aware of it. Dad always kept that as a separate entity, completely self-sufficient, and independent from his legal business," John explained.

"So what do you think I should do now?" John asked Mike.

"Well, the first thing you should do is swear out a warrant for Samuels' arrest for grand theft and embezzlement.

"Second, if you were anyone else I would suggest hiring an attorney to recover your property," Mike suggested.

"I know who I can hire, if he will agree to do it. My old college professor named Professor Moriarity has the best legal mind I know of, besides my dad," John replied.

"Sounds good. Now let's go back to my office and get the ball rolling. I also will have to get the names of your parent's murderers, so I can start looking for them," Mike said.

At the office John gave Mike the names of Indian Bob and Caleb and Carl Keegan and everything he knew about them.

Then John told Mike, "I'm going to be out of town for some time. I have to go check on Maria and Lisa. Then I'll go to the ranch to see Juan Ortiz and go to Austin and see if I can hire Professor Moriarity," John told him.

"Just be careful and check in with me when you get back," Mike warned.

His first stop was at Maria's house, and it was empty with a "For Rent" sign on it. Then he went to Lisa's house and was greeted at the door by Maria and Lisa.

"Oh, John, how good to see you," Maria said.

Lisa added, "Thank God you are safe. What in the world happened?"

"Well, Dad's former partner, David Samuels, stole everything from me," John replied.

"And how is Sarah?" Lisa asked.

"Still no change. She is still in a coma, and what is worse, Samuels never paid a penny for her hospital care. If it hadn't been for Mike Ward they would have moved her to the county charity hospital," John reported.

"But how are you two?"

"We are surviving. We received no notice or severance pay. We couldn't find another job so we moved in together to save money," Lisa reported.

John spoke next, "It is terrible what an evil man can accomplish in just six weeks, but I will make sure he is punished one way or another."

"Just be careful. We will survive, but we need for you to be safe," Maria said.

John told them, "I will be OK. I was able to take some cash from

Dad's safe, and that will tide me over until I get my property back. He opened his money belt where he kept the money from the safe. Then he handed each of them two ten-dollar gold pieces, saying, "I hope this will hold you over until I get back on my feet again."

"You are a generous young man. Thank you so much," Lisa said.

Saying "You're welcome," John left for the ranch.

John arrived at the ranch by early evening and was greeted warmly by Juan Ortiz.

"John, boy, I'm so glad to see you. I have been wondering what happened to everyone. I heard what happened to your mom and dad and Sarah, but no one was able to tell me anything about you."

John sat down with Juan, drank a beer and filled him in on everything that occurred over the past two months.

"*Mucho malo*," Juan said, "What happened to Lisa and Maria?"

"They're living together at Lisa's house and can't find other jobs."

"Well, I could sure use them here. The cook is so terrible the ranch hands are complaining about the food. He is a *gringo* and can't cook the Mexican food the men like. Also I have been doing without a cook and housekeeper. I have been eating with the hands at every meal, and that is not good. After a while they think I am just one of them and won't take orders from me," Juan reported.

"I understand," John said.

"Give me their address, and I'll take one of the hands with me and move them here tomorrow," Juan told him.

Juan made them both sandwiches, which they ate, drank another *cerveza,* and went to bed.

The next morning John left early and headed for Austin. He had to wait until class was finished then met with Professor Moriarity.

John greeted him, "Hello, Professor Moriarity."

"John King, is that you?" Moriarity surprisingly asked.

"Yes indeed," John answered.

"What happened to you? The last time I saw you, you were dressed like a college student, and now you show up here looking like a hired killer."

"Sorry to surprise you, Professor," John said. "Can you spare some time for me?"

"Of course, but only if you call me Marvin. I am not your professor anymore," he replied.

"Yes, sir," John agreed.

They sat down in Moriarity's office, and John filled him in on what had happened since he left school.

"I'm sorry about your problems, son, but how can I be of assistance?" Moriarity asked.

"You can use your great legal mind to help me get my property back."

"You mean you want to hire me as a lawyer?" Moriarity asked.

"Yes sir, that is exactly what I mean," John answered.

"How much money is involved?" the professor wanted to know.

"Over one million and slightly under two million," John answered.

Moriarity whistled softly and said, "You know the usual recovery fee is ten percent."

"Yes sir, I am aware of that, and I am willing to pay that to get you," John said.

Moriarity said, "In that case, I accept. I can take a sabbatical, move in with a lady friend I know in Houston, and meet with you next Monday morning. Where can we meet?"

"Thank you, sir. I'll meet you at the Houston Police Station in Chief Ward's office at eight in the morning on Monday," John said.

The deal done, they shook hands, and John left the campus. He thought to himself, *As long as I'm in Austin, and I don't have a home in Houston to go to, I might as well look up my old girlfriend, Lola.*

He rode to Lola's apartment and knocked on the door. She answered wearing a loose-fitting house frock.

"Is that you, John King?"

"In the flesh," John answered.

"Then get in here and kiss me," she said.

John gladly obliged, and then he had to tell his story again to eager and anxious ears.

"You poor thing. I am so sorry for your problems, but thanks for sharing them with me," she said.

She fixed both of them a drink, and told him, "I am so glad you're here. Life has been so boring without you."

"Well I'm here for a couple of days and I'll try and make sure you don't get bored," John teasingly said.

"Where are you staying?" Lola asked.

"Here, if you'll let me," he answered.

"That would be heavenly. I hope you will stay with me," she said as she began pulling of his boots.

As she did John enjoyed the sight of her exposed small breasts peering out from the house frock. He began to get aroused. It had been a long time since he had been with a woman.

It had been a long time for her, too. First she removed his vest, then his shirt. John helped by removing his gun belt and she began tugging on his jeans to get them off. Then John started pulling the frock over her head and discovered she was wearing nothing underneath.

"Damn, you look good," he blurted out.

"So do you," she said and began kissing him all over his body.

After that they made love right there on the sofa, both of them too anxious to even make it to the bedroom.

It was a brief lovemaking session. It took hardly any time for both of them to be satisfied, they both having been so horny for it. When they were finished, John whispered, "Oh, Lola, thank you so much. That was so wonderful."

"Don't go thanking me yet; this class is not dismissed yet! This will be the longest class you were ever in," Lola answered.

Lola then got up and made them both another drink, without bothering to put on her smock. John admired her graceful body as he thought, *My luck is rapidly changing for the better.*

Before they had even finished their second drink, Lola whispered in John's ear, "Make love to me again darling, and I'll fix us a light supper."

"It's a deal," he said as he took her by the hand and led her into the bedroom.

They did make love again, but this time it took a little longer but was just as satisfying. This time Lola took him by the hand and led him to the table. She said, "You sit here, I'll fix you another drink, and while you are drinking it I'll fix us something to eat."

In what seemed no time, Lola had fixed two plates of macaroni salad and tuna sandwiches. They both ate ravenously, their appetites aroused by the horizontal exercises. After their hunger for food was satisfied, they returned to the sofa to talk.

John asked, "What do you have to do tomorrow?"

"Absolutely nothing. If I had classes, which I don't, I would cut them and stay here with you," she replied.

"Then how about if we get drunk tonight, sleep late, and make love all day tomorrow?" John asked.

"I'm game if you are," she replied.

They didn't get drunk, but they did have one more drink, went to bed, made love again, and then slept until eight o'clock in the morning. Lola let John sleep a few minutes longer as she got up, made coffee, and took a cup to John while he was still in bed.

They sat on the bed and sipped coffee as they talked. Lola asked, "Do you have to leave today?"

"I'm afraid so. I have to be in Houston for an eight a.m. meeting Monday, so I'll have to leave this morning," John answered.

"I wish you could stay longer," Lola offered.

"Believe me, I would love to enjoy this kind of treatment a little while longer. The last two months have been nothing but work, worry, tension, and stress, and I am worn out with it," John answered.

Lola fixed him ham, eggs, and biscuits, then kissed him as he dressed to leave.

Lola walked with him to his horse, kissed him, and said, "Please come back soon."

"I will, and as soon as I find a place to live I'll send you a wire and invite you to come and spend a weekend at my place. Can you do that?"

"Of course I can, and I will," she responded. John kissed her, hard, and rode off for Houston.

It was late when he reached the outskirts of Houston, so he checked into a hotel, cared for Diablo, then went to his room to get a bath, a good night's sleep, and to prepare for his meeting the next morning. By six the next morning he was on Diablo and en route to Mike Ward's office.

When he walked in, he found Mike and Moriarity waiting for him.

Moriarity got right down to business asking what was in the illegally opened safe. John used his amazing memory to recite the safe's contents including the list of securities, including the amounts of each security, even reciting the serial numbers. Moriarity told him, "I see your memory hasn't started failing you."

"I'll take it from here," the professor said.

"Who will you go after first?" Mike asked John.

"That depends on who you have information on," John answered him.

"Nothing on Samuels or the Keegan brothers, but I discovered a big stack of wanted posters on Indian Bob. He is one mean son of a bitch. Last week he shot two deputies in the back at Galveston. They were trying to guard a cargo boat carrying liquor, and he caught them off-guard and killed them. Then he and two accomplices stole an entire wagon load of scotch whiskey."

"Suppose the Keegans helped him?" John asked.

"Could be. Nobody identified his cronies," Mike answered him.

"Why don't you let me ask the Texas Rangers to help you?" Mike asked.

"No thanks. They don't know me, and I'll have a better chance of sneaking up on them if I don't have rangers with me," John responded.

John rode toward Galveston but decided to stop by the ranch on the way. He found Lisa and Maria all settled in and happy to be working at the ranch.

Deciding to try a little deception, John found one of his dad's suits and changed into it. It fit him fairly well but was a little large in the waist and a little short in the legs; still, John thought it would serve the purpose.

Chapter 5
John Meets the Killers

In Galveston he went from bar to bar, identifying himself as a saloon owner from San Antonio looking to buy some cheap liquor. Two days he did this and finally was contacted by a shady looking character who told him he could get his hands on some cheap scotch.

"That's a start, but I need bourbon too," John said, trying to act not real interested.

The stranger told him, "Well, I know I can get the scotch now and bourbon later."

"How much?" John asked.

"Twenty-five cents a bottle as much as you want to buy," came the answer.

John said, "I will need a sample, and if I like it I'll take 800 bottles." All this time he was wondering if he was negotiating with one of the Keegans.

The stranger introduced himself as Clay Collins. John remembered Clay was also the name of the Keegan brothers.

They agreed to meet the following day at noon on Pier 3 at the docks.

Clay told him, "You bring the money, and I'll bring a sample of the scotch."

"Oh, no, I didn't just fall off of a wagon load of turnips. I'll taste the sample and if I like it, I'll give you the money when I get the merchandise," John said.

Clay agreed and John returned to his hotel room, hoping all went well tomorrow. The next morning John had biscuits and gravy in the hotel dining room, then got his horse and rode to the agreed meeting place, a house about five miles from town. Upon arrival, he saw that two other men were with Clay. One of them resembled Clay and the other was obviously an Indian. John thought to himself, *I hit the jackpot. No doubt these are the Keegan brothers and Indian Bob. Be alert and watch yourself.*

"You bring the money?" Clay asked.

"Where's the merchandise?" John asked.

The Indian opened the door to the next room and there on the floor were 80 boxes, each containing ten bottles of scotch.

"Now show me the money," Clay demanded.

"I left it at the hotel. I'll go back and rent a wagon to move the whiskey and bring the money back with me," John told him.

"You're a liar. The money is not at the hotel. We searched your room this morning," Clay sneered.

"I told you yesterday, I didn't fall off a wagon load of turnips. The money is in the hotel safe. I wouldn't leave that much money lying around," John said.

The Indian said, "He lies. Search him."

"Oh no, I told you I'll bring the money," John angrily replied.

What happened after that was, at best, a blurred memory. John felt pain on the left side of his head then pain in his left arm. He vaguely remembered emptying his Peacemaker at the three, then drawing and firing his Lightning, then complete darkness.

Left for dead, he awoke in about half an hour. Both Keegans were dead, and there was blood where Indian Bob had been standing. To be sure the Keegans were both dead, John reloaded his Peacemaker and shot the Keegans again in the head. Other than the blood on the floor there was no sign of Indian Bob.

John then wrapped his bandana around the wound on his head. Luckily a bullet had only creased his head. Then he looked at his arm; it hurt like hell and was bleeding profusely. He remembered reading about how to stop bleeding by cauterizing the wound, so he removed the bullet from one of the .45 cartridges and emptied the powder on the wound. He lit the powder with a match. He felt pain like he had never felt before but the bleeding lessened, then stopped. He could barely stand but he somehow got through the door and managed to drag himself onto Diablo. Hoping he didn't pass out from blood loss, he rode to Galveston, first to the doctor's office, then to the police department.

All the way to town John kept thinking to himself, *Damn it, damn it. I had all three of them and let Indian Bob get away.*

As it turned out, he didn't have to go to the police station. Dr. Adams took one look at him and sent for the police.

Dr. Adams told John, "You were lucky son. Your scalp was grazed slightly, and the shot to your arm missed the bone. Your head will heal in a few days but your arm will be only partly unusable for a couple of weeks."

Jim Kline was the police officer who questioned John about his injuries. As he talked, John felt for his money belt, and it was still there. That was the reason he didn't want to be searched.

John identified himself, and then related the entire story to Officer Kline and Dr. Adams. Kline carefully took notes for the report he had to file, and then asked John why he was after those men.

John told him, "Those three bastards killed my parents and beat and raped my sister, who now is just a vegetable."

Kline said, "Oh yes, I read about that in the paper, but you shouldn't have gone up against them alone."

"You're right. Chief Ward in Houston wanted me to bring some rangers with me, but I was too stubborn to listen to him," John admitted.

Then John asked Kline to send a wire to Houston and inform Chief Ward of today's happenings.

Then John told Kline, "If you will go out to the house where it happened I think you will find the Keegans and some of the scotch whiskey they stole."

Kline told John, "I'll send the wire first then go out there right away."

"Better take someone with you in case Indian Bob is still hanging around," John warned him.

"Thanks, I will, but I hope the son of a bitch is still there," Kline responded.

Then Dr. Adams told John, "You won't be able to travel for a couple of days. You can stay here today and tonight. I'll have someone tend to your horse, and we'll see how you feel in the morning."

"Thanks Doc. I can pay you," John said.

"Money is the last thing on my mind right now. I just want to make sure those wounds of yours don't start bleeding again," Doc Adams reminded him.

Alone for a few minutes, John fell into a deep sleep, weak from the loss of blood, and stunned by the day's events. He had never killed anyone before, but he vowed he would still try to kill Indian Bob, then Samuels.

Without realizing it, John slept for four hours even lying on the hard examination table. He was awakened by Kline, who told him they found the bodies of the Keegans and the liquor. He said a stray shot had ripped through the boxes of scotch, and liquor was all over the floor.

He also reported the chief had a return wire from Mike Ward asking them to take John to his ranch west of town, and thanking them for looking after his friend.

John told him, "I would appreciate a ride to the ranch, but first I'll need to check out of the hotel. I would appreciate it if you would go there with me. Indian Bob knows where I was staying, and I fear he may be there waiting for me."

"Of course I'll go with you, and I hope the dirty bastard is there. I would be happy to kill him for you," Kline said.

Kline checked the room first, and then told John it was OK to enter. John went in, changed into his black clothes, threw away his Dad's ruined suit, and then checked out.

The two of them rode in the buggy to the ranch, John's horse tied to the buggy.

On the way, Kline said, "Oh, John, I almost forgot, there was a $250 bounty on each of the Keegans, so you have $500 coming. Pretty easy money, huh?"

"I would rather not have the money and not been shot. I didn't do it for the money. Please tell the chief to mail it to me at the ranch," John told him.

"Will do," Kline answered.

John was still weak so Kline helped him into the ranch house where he was mobbed by Juan, Maria, and Lisa. John explained what had transpired and Juan helped him into his bed, saying he would spend the night in the bunk house.

Lisa and Maria fussed over him as if he were their child with a skinned knee. Juan thanked Kline, took charge of Diablo, and Kline rode off to Galveston.

John rested up for three days as the girls changed his bandages, cooked for him, and nursed him back to health. His wounds were almost healed, but he still kept his left arm in a sling to keep pressure off of his wound.

It was Friday morning when John had unexpected visitors. Professor Moriarity and Chief Ward rode up in a buggy.

Moriarity and Ward greeted him warmly, Mike Ward calling him the wounded warrior. John learned the two of them had become friends while working together trying to unravel the mess created by Samuels. Moriarity gave John good news: "I'm happy to tell you I got your house and office building back for you," he said.

"How did you ever do that so fast?" John asked.

"That was relatively easy. Samuels is not so smart after all. Instead of hiring a good forger, he apparently counterfeited your signature himself. The judge only had to compare the signatures on the two deeds, and he laughed out loud. Then he issued a court order deeding both of them back to you," Moriarity reported.

"Thank you, sir," John told him.

Then Mike Ward spoke up, "I have good news for you too. Here is a voucher for $500, as reward for killing the two Keegan brothers."

"But I already got a reward for them from the City of Galveston," John said.

"This reward is from the State of Texas, who wanted them for murder. That other reward was for the recovery of the scotch whiskey," Ward explained.

"I didn't know bounty hunting could be so profitable," John chuckled.

"Yeah, it is if you live long enough, and you almost didn't," Mike said.

After having lunch Maria and Lisa fixed for them, John, Moriarity and Mike left for Houston in the buggy, with Diablo tethered behind.

During the trip, Mike asked John, "Where do you plan to live?"

"I hadn't thought much about it, but even if I have my parents' house back, I couldn't very well live there, with no furniture and no help," John told him.

"Well, the reason I asked is that a new residence hotel just opened up. It is called the Wedgewood. They have a small café in it but no bar. It is for people who want the conveniences of a hotel but plan on staying there permanently. I hear it even has an attended stable for the horses of guests," Mike told him.

"Sounds like just what I need for the time being," John answered.

Then Moriarity interrupted, "If you don't want to do that, I'm sure my lady friend Shirley would be happy to have you stay with her until you get back on your feet."

"That would be nice of her, but I wouldn't think of putting her out," John answered.

"Well, I still have a lot of work to do tracking down your stocks and bonds. That Samuels fellow traded all of them for bearer bonds, which means he can cash them anywhere. But I will recover them for you; it will just take a little more time. Of course that means I'll have to stay in Houston a lot longer, but I am liking staying with Shirley anyways," Moriarity confessed to them.

Mike and John laughed.

Mike and Moriarity waited in the buggy while John went in to check out the Wedgewood. After a few minutes they knew John had rented a room there when an attendant emerged, retrieved John's horse, and took him to the stable.

Then John came out saying, "Thanks for waiting. I took a room there. I like it a lot. Professor, I guess you can go ahead with your idea of selling the house and office building. I think this place will do nicely."

Saying their good-byes and accepting John's thanks, they left. John spent the rest of the day napping and getting a bath. The next morning he had breakfast in the small café in the hotel. The attendant had saddled Diablo, and John rode to St. Agnes Hospital to see Sarah.

A smiling Sister Ruth greeted him at the door. *Damn, she's too pretty to be a nun*, John thought.

"Hello, John. God bless you," she greeted him.

"Thank you, Sister. How is Sarah?" John asked.

"Well, earlier this week we had a glimmer of hope when she opened her eyes for a few minutes, but then she lapsed back into unconsciousness," she responded.

Upon seeing his sister lying there, he wanted to cry but instead replaced his grief with rage, and repeated his promise to get even with Indian Bob, the only one left of the original four.

He sat by her bedside and talked to her as if she could hear him, "Dear Sarah, I found the Keegins and killed them, and I almost had the Indian but he got away. But I promise you I will get him, too."

Feeling like he might cry again, John left.

He first rode to the telegram office where he sent a telegram to Lola.

He advised her of his new address and invited her to visit him, when and if she got a chance.

Then he rode to the police station. He told Mike he planned on taking some time off, then going after Indian Bob. A return telegram from Lola was waiting for him when he returned to the Wedgewood. She asked him to meet the Thursday train and she would be on it. He thought, *It will be good to see her, have a little fun, and have someone to change the bandages for me.*

Thursday morning John got up early, had breakfast at the hotel restaurant, then retrieved his horse and went shopping for some wine, good bourbon, and a gift for Lola. He decided to get her a silver bracelet with a single silver heart on which he had engraved "Lola," then he met the train.

As soon as she spotted John, Lola ran to him, kissed him and blurted out, "John, you've been wounded. What happened?"

"Let's go to my place first and have a drink. Then I'll tell you all about it."

Lola had questions during the buggy ride to the hotel, but John remained vague until he could relate the entire story.

Lola made herself at home and poured each of them a large bourbon, then said, "Now, you tell me all about how you got hurt."

"I will sweetheart, but first, before I forget, let me reimburse you for your train ticket," he told her.

Lola's mood instantly turned sour as she said angrily, "Reimburse me? Reimburse me--what do you think I am, some whore you can pay to come and have sex with you?"

"No, oh no, that is not how I meant it. I know most college students don't have a lot of extra money," John said, trying to apologize.

Still sounding angry, Lola said, "John, I guess we never talked about this before, but my daddy is one of the richest men in Dallas. He is president of Bigelow Oil, and my mother, Bambi, inherited the biggest feed lot in Fort Worth. I have an older brother Sully, but I am their only daughter. They give me more money that I can spend."

"Er, um, I'm so sorry," John stammered, still trying to apologize.

Lola finally calmed down and said, "OK, let's just forget it. I am here because you do things to me that make me feel good, and because I like you."

John took her in his arms and told her, "Lola, I like you, too, and the things you do to me make me feel good too. Now let's have another drink."

"I'll fix the drinks and you tell me all about how you were wounded," Lola said.

John told her the entire story about the Keegans, Indian Bob, and the stolen whiskey. Neither of them finished their second drink, but they held hands, walked to the bed, undressed each other, and then got into bed to make up as lovers have done since the beginning of time.

For the next three days Lola cooked for him, changed his bandages, and made love whenever one or both of them wanted to. This routine lasted for three days; they did not leave the room and even declined maid service when it was offered.

On the fourth day John was feeling much better. He drove Lola to the depot so she could take the train to San Antonio and the stage coach to Austin.

After they kissed good-bye John asked, "Need any money for the train ticket?"

She hit him hard on his unwounded arm; it hurt. Then they both laughed and kissed again.

Then she boarded the train, took a seat by a window, and waved until John disappeared from view.

Then John decided to go to see Mike Ward at the police station. As if they were expecting him, Moriarity and Ward were together talking as John walked in.

Moriarity spoke first, "John, we both have news for you."

"Good or bad?" John asked.

"I guess some of both," Mike added.

Moriarity volunteered, "I have some good news for you. We tracked Samuels down through the sales of the bearer bonds. The last ones were cashed in Monterrey, Mexico, so if you want to look for him that would be a good place to start. Also I sold your house and office building for a good price. The funds have been deposited in the State Bank of Houston.

"I also used some of the funds to set up a trust fund for Sarah, so her future care is provided for. I told Sister Ruth about it, and she asked about you."

"Thank you, sir. I knew I could trust you," John told him.

Then Mike reported, "This is probably good and bad news. Indian Bob is in jail in El Paso."

"What happened?" John excitedly asked.

"Well, it seems he passed out on the stage coach due to loss of blood from a nasty stomach wound. Some good Samaritans took him to the hospital there, but when he came to, he tried to kill them. The sheriff arrested him and threw him in jail. Then he recognized him from a wanted poster and sent me a telegram saying he would hold him for me. I'm making arrangements now to send some men out there to bring him back," Mike told him.

"Better send some good men. He is one mean bastard and would do anything to escape," John warned him.

"Don't worry, I'll send two of my best cops and they will bring him back," Mike assured him.

"I sure hope they do, but I will worry about them until he is safely in prison," John told Mike.

Moriarity then announced, "I will be leaving tomorrow. Got to get back to the mundane existence of a college professor."

John asked him, "What about your bill? I owe you quite a bit of money, not to mention a great deal of thanks."

"Just wait until you catch Samuels and we'll find out how much money he has left, then I'll mail you a bill," Moriarity told him.

"Thank you sir, and please give my best to Lola Bigelow when you see her," John said.

"I will do that," the professor answered.

The next morning John left early for the ranch. He hoped to get Juan to go with him to Monterrey to find Samuels. At the ranch he was greeted warmly by Lisa and Maria, then Juan. They were all glad to see him healthy again.

Then John asked Juan, "Would you be able to go to Monterrey with me for a few weeks?"

"*Si, Senor*, I can teach Lisa and Maria to make the payroll, and the rest of the ranch can run itself for a few weeks, but what is going on?" Juan answered.

"Well, a paper trail of Daddy's money tracked Samuels to Monterrey, and I want to go there and either arrest him or kill him," John explained.

"OK, I'll go. But I won't help you kill anyone," Juan commented. I have family in Monterrey, and I would like to see them while I'm there."

Then Lisa offered a suggestion, "Why don't you two ride the new train from Corpus Christi to Laredo?"

"What train?" Juan and John asked, almost in unison.

"Maria and I heard about it at the market. It is a new train that runs from Corpus Christi to Laredo, then on to Monterrey," Lisa explained.

"That sounds like a good idea, and we can borrow some horses from my cousin if we need to," Juan said.

The next morning Maria drove Juan and John to Corpus Christi after packing a big basket of sandwiches for them to eat on the train.

After they got on board they learned the train was a joint venture between the Kansas City Southern Railroad and the Mexican Railroad. When they left Corpus Christi the crew would be a Kansas City Southern crew, but at Laredo a Mexican Railroad crew would take over and take the train on to Monterrey.

Although it had been a long day on the train, at least they saved themselves two or three days in the saddle. They also discussed that if they were able to apprehend Samuels, the train would be an easy way to get him back to Texas to stand trial.

It was almost dark when they arrived at the station in Monterrey.

At the station they noticed a large police presence. Three armed policemen patrolled in and around the station.

Juan explained they were there to guard unsuspecting travelers. Some women had been the victims of local *pachukas* robbing them. Male travelers were often solicited by the local *putas* plying their trade.

It was too late to visit John's cousins that night, so after eating supper at a small diner they checked into a boarding house called *Casa de Flores* close to the station. They were both tired from the trip and were soon sound asleep in a not-too-comfortable bed. They were too tired to care. It had been a long day.

The next morning after coffee at the boarding house, Juan inquired after a livery stable but Senora Flores volunteered to take them to Juan's cousin's house. As they rode to the address given to Senora Flores, John spent his time looking at his surroundings. He had been told about and had read about Mexico's caste system, but now he was observing it firsthand.

He saw a small stream flowing through a large settlement of shacks and huts. All had dirt floors. The upstream part of the river was used by the women and children to dip water and carry it back to the small huts. The middle sections of the stream were used by women washing clothes by beating them on rocks. The lower part of the stream was used as a sewer, judging from the stench.

At least they know that much about sanitation, John thought to himself.

As they left the downtown area and climbed a hill John couldn't help but notice the huge contrast in houses. At the top of the hill they were suddenly in a neighborhood of very large houses surrounded by stone, adobe, and brick walls. Atop the walls were barbed wire and broken glass.

Juan directed Senora Flores to a large gate with a sign that said "ORTIZ" in the center. Juan thanked Senora Flores, gave her $5.00, and then pulled the rope on a large bell atop the gate.

The bell was answered by another Mexican man and Juan told him, in Spanish, his name and that he was looking for his cousin Tomas and his wife, Rosita.

They were allowed to enter and walked past several out buildings on the way to the main brick house. Juan explained to John one of the buildings was a stable, one a servant's quarters, and one a guest house.

They were led into the main house and were greeted warmly by Tomas and Rosita. Both of Juan's relatives were approaching middle age. Tomas had salt and pepper hair, dark skin, and blue eyes. He stood barely more than five feet tall and had the build of an athlete.

Rosita was a beautiful woman with skin lighter than her husband, and was at least six inches taller. Her hair was brown, and she had large blue eyes. She still maintained a beautiful shape. Her large breasts were still the focal point for most men's glances.

They were served a wonderfully-tasting lunch of tamales and rice and beans with tortillas. Juan and John ate with gusto, as this was their first meal of the day. That afternoon the four of them sat in the parlor exchanging pleasantries and explaining the purpose of their visit.

John had been wondering how the Ortiz couple had achieved their wealth. Not being able to stand it any longer he finally said, "Please excuse me for asking a rude question, but did you two inherit all of this?"

Rosita and Tomas both laughed loudly in unison, "Not hardly!"

"We both came from very poor families," Tomas continued. "My parents raised me on a small goat farm about ten miles from here. Rosita was raised on a small farm nearby and she and all of her brothers and sisters worked in the fields."

Then Rosita added, "We would probably still be doing that if God had not shed His grace on us and showed us a path out of poverty."

Then Tomas took over the story: "Rosita and I were childhood friends, and I think we loved each other when we were seven or eight years old."

Rosita smiled and gently stroked Tomas' face.

"Anyway, Rosita learned to make salsa when she was a teenager," Tomas continued.

"It was my grandmother's recipe," Rosita interrupted.

Then Tomas resumed the story, "She would make large batches in a kettle over an open fire. People would come for miles around to buy small jars of it for five *centavos*, and some days she would sell out the entire batch. After this went on for months, I convinced her she should make larger batches and I would take jars into town and sell them. Soon Rosita's Salsa became the talk of the entire town. That is when I borrowed money from my parents, added it to money Rosita had saved, and we moved here and set up a small factory. To make a long story short, the business grew and expanded. Our salsa business thrived, and within five years we sold the business to a company from San Antonio for more money than we knew existed."

"Wow, that is some success story," Juan commented.

"Well, it's all true," Tomas assured him.

"But now, enough of our story; tell us about yourself," Rosita said.

So John related the story of his parent's murder, his sister's rape, and the theft of his property by his father's ex-partner.

"Now I am here trying to track down bonds at a bank here. And I thought I might find him here," John told them.

"What bank did he use?" Tomas asked.

John took a piece of paper from his shirt pocket, unfolded it and handed it to Tomas. It read:

Banco de Mexico, De *Monterrey*

Tomas excitedly said, "That's the bank I use. I know all of the people there, and if you want me to I'll go there with you tomorrow."

After a breakfast of *huevos rancheros* and tortillas, Tomas drove John and Juan to the bank. As they parked the buggy in front Tomas told them, "If you don't mind I'll go in alone. I know most of the people, and they will talk more freely if I am alone."

Tomas returned in just a few minutes.

Chapter 6
The Search for Samuels Begins

Tomas emerged triumphantly from the bank announcing, "I think we've got the bastard. They don't know anyone named Samuels, but a man calling himself Romeo Jacobs cashed $10,000 worth of bearer bonds two weeks ago. Here is his address."

And he handed a piece of paper which read "Romeo Jacobs, 1313 Buena Vista, Monterrey."

"Do you know where that is?" John asked.

"*Si senor*, and I'll take you there now, if you like," Tomas replied.

"Then let's go get the son of a bitch," John said loudly.

Tomas drove past the address, then parked a half block away. He suggested, "Let me go up and knock on the door, and if he's there I'll signal you and you can come and get him."

"Sounds good," Juan said, the excitement showing in his voice.

To everyone's surprise the door was answered by a young Mexican girl of 16 or 17. She spoke very broken English but agreed to bring Romeo to the door. Tomas signaled, and John and Juan walked slowly toward the house, not wanting to draw attention to themselves.

Seeing them coming, Samuels attempted to retreat into the house but Tomas grabbed him in a choke hold and held him until John and Juan arrived. The Mexican girl screamed and ran into the house.

They forced Samuels into the house where John held him at gunpoint as he searched him. He found and removed a Remington derringer from his vest pocket and Colt pocket pistol from a shoulder holster.

Samuels was visibly shaken but asked, "Why are you robbing me?"

"Robbing you? You better hope I don't kill you right where you stand, you thieving bastard," John told him.

Still belligerent Samuels said, "I'm going to have you arrested."

"Please try and do that, you son of a bitch, and I'll kill you before they get here, and I mean I really will. It's all I can do to keep from killing you right now, for all the grief you have brought on me," John threatened.

As John was talking to Samuels, Juan and Tomas were questioning the young Mexican girl, who told them her name was Carmen.

Then John asked Samuels, "OK, now where are the rest of the bearer bonds and the cash you got for the ones you cashed at the bank?"

"None of your business," Samuels snarled.

"OK, you bastard. I was hoping to do this the easy way, but we can do it the hard way. I'm going to shoot you in one knee cap and you will limp for life. Then if you haven't told me, I'll shoot you in the other knee cap and you will spend the rest of your life in a wheel chair. Then if you haven't told me I'll put you out of your misery with a bullet through the roof of your mouth. Now let's get started," John threatened, drew his pistol, and pointed it at Samuel's right knee.

Samuels quickly lost his arrogance and began to sweat.

"OK, OK, don't shoot. I'll tell you," he said.

"You have ten seconds to hand over the bonds and cash, or I'll start shooting, and if you think I'm lying, look in my eyes," John told him.

Samuels stared into John's eyes and saw nothing but hate.

John followed Samuels closely as he went into the bedroom and took a briefcase from under the bed and laid it on the bed.

John warned him, "Just unlock it; don't reach inside. I'll do that."

John's caution paid off. When he opened the case another Colt pocket pistol was on top of a pile of cash and bonds. John told him, "You're not only a damned thief, but a sneak too. I should just kill you right now. I could be back in Texas before anyone finds you. In fact, I think I will just kill you now," and he reached for a pillow as if to muffle the sound. Samuels not only was sweating more, but he began to tremble. He was sure he was about to die. Indeed the thought had crossed John's mind but he thought better of it.

Samuels started to think he would live when John produced a set of shackles and fastened them on Samuel's wrists behind his back.

Samuels complained, "They are too tight. They are hurting my wrists."

"Good," John said.

The buggy only held four, so John fashioned a noose from a rope. He put the noose around Samuels's throat and forced him to walk behind the buggy. His hands were still shackled behind his back. Tomas, Juan, John and Carmen rode in the crowded buggy. John held the briefcase on his lap and one hand held the rope tethered to Samuels.

Samuels complained loudly all of the way then John shouted to him, "You shut up, or I'll have them speed up the wagon and drag you by the neck."

Samuels quieted down. Traveling through the poor section of town, several people came out into the street to watch them pass by. A few old women knelt down and crossed themselves. They thought they were watching a crude reenactment of Jesus carrying the cross.

When they got back to the Ortiz home, Tomas helped John lock Samuels in the stable tack room. He then instructed his most trusted employee, Jose Ramos, to guard him. Jose sat on a bale of hay outside the locked tack room door with a Winchester rifle across his lap. Tomas explained to John, "He will be secure in there. Jose is my most honest employee, and he knows how to use that rifle. Every year I give him time off to hunt deer with his friends, and every year he brings us venison."

The rest of them went into the house to hear Carmen's story. Juan and Tomas took turns relating the story Carmen told them earlier.

Her parents were killed when a mud slide pushed their buggy over a cliff on a road outside of Mexico City. Her only living relative was an uncle, so she was sent here to live with him. Unfortunately her uncle had no interest in girls or women. He and his live-in partner, Pedro, only loved each other. After her uncle met Samuels in some *cantina*, he sold her to Samuels for $50 in American money.

Samuels was mean to her. He literally made a slave of her. She did all of the cooking and cleaning. She was beaten if he was drunk or refused his commands to perform kinky sex acts with him. Hearing this, Rosita rushed to her, hugged and kissed her and told her in Spanish, "You poor dear, you are safe here. You can live with us, and we will take care of you and treat you like you were our own daughter."

Carmen smiled and said, "*Gracias, gracias.*"

Then Tomas volunteered, "That may be something else you can pin on Samuels."

"What is that?" John asked.

"Slavery and false imprisonment. If you will guard Samuels for a while, I'll send Jose to bring my attorney here. He can take a deposition from her, have her sign it, I'll witness it, and you can use that at his trial," Tomas suggested.

"Great idea. And if it's OK with you, I'll ask Juan to go into town with him and send a telegram to the ranch and have them meet us in Corpus Christi with a wagon."

"Fine, fine," answered Tomas. In about an hour Jose and Juan returned with the attorney, Pablo Fuentes, following in his own buggy.

Tomas made introductions all around then Pablo and Carmen adjourned to a quiet library to prepare her deposition. The ever efficient attorney first took her deposition in Spanish, wrote it down exactly as she said it, then promptly translated it and wrote it down in English.

When he and Carmen returned everyone was enjoying a pitcher of margaritas and he joined them saying, "After hearing about him, I am glad I don't have to defend him. He is Satan in disguise. I'd like to have a look at him before I go home."

John took Pablo to the tack room and granted his wish to see the prisoner. Samuels showed little emotion when the door was opened. He just finished eating the dinner Tomas had brought to him.

Pablo looked him in the eyes, and then turned away. He told Juan later Samuels was too evil to look at very long.

The next morning Tomas took Juan, John, and Samuels, still in manacles, to the train station.

John and Juan both thanked Tomas. John told his hosts he would like to return to the ranch sometime soon, so they could return the hospitality by having them visit his ranch in the future. Tomas indicated he would take them up on the offer.

During the long train ride John and Juan took turns napping and alternated guarding Samuels.

When they finally arrived in Corpus Christi they looked for Lisa and Maria. Instead they found Chief Ward, and two men John did not know.

Mike Ward introduced them to Officer Winters and Assistant Police Chief Joe Alexander.

Alexander and Winters re-shackled Samuels, handed John his manacles, and hustled the prisoner out of ear shot as Mike talked to John. But before they took him away John said, "Wait just a minute. I have one more thing to say to him. "Samuels, you low-life bastard. It wasn't bad enough you stole millions from my dad's estate, but the worst thing you did was refuse to set up a trust fund for my sister, Sarah. If it hadn't been for Chief Ward they would have moved her to a charity hospital. I will be there to testify to that at your trial."

Samuels looked at the ground as he was led away.

Then Mike's face reddened as he told John, "I have some really bad news for you. Indian Bob has escaped."

"Oh, shit. What happened?" John asked.

Mike replied, "Oh, shit is right. And he killed two of my best officers in the process. They were also close friends of mine, so now I have a personal stake in catching that animal."

"How did that come about?" John wanted to know.

"Well, apparently some good Samaritans found him unconscious on a train and took him to a doctor's office where he tried to kill them. The doctor sent for the sheriff, who arrested him. The sheriff recognized him from a wanted poster, but Bob was acting so wild the doctor wasn't able to dig the bullet out of him.

"In the confusion he must have stolen a scalpel from the doctor's office and concealed it on himself somehow."

"Where did he escape?" John inquired.

Mike continued, "According to the report I got from the conductor, one of the officers went to relieve himself while the train was loading cargo in San Antonio. Somehow he slipped out of his wrist shackles, retrieved the scalpel, and slit the throat of one officer. Then he took the pistol from the officer's body and shot the other officer when he returned. That's why I'm meeting you here instead of the ranch, so I can get a head start hunting him. Want to go with me?"

"You bet your ass I do," John eagerly replied.

Chapter 7
The Search for Indian Bob

"**I** thought you might; that's why I brought your horse along with mine," Mike told him.

John took the briefcase, handed it to Juan, and told him, "Juan, lock this up in the ranch safe until I get back. I'm going with Mike to bring back Indian Bob, dead or alive but preferably dead."

"*Si senor,*" Juan told him, and they all watched as Mike and John rode away.

As they rode off to the northwest, John asked Mike, "Where do we start to look for him?

"Well, I figure he will try to get to the Indian Nation where he thinks he can hide out. With that slug still in him, where you shot him, I doubt that he will be able to do the 'Apache Shuffle' for very long, so he'll probably try to steal a horse," Mike said.

"What is the 'Apache Shuffle'?" John asked.

"The 'Apache Shuffle' is something all young Apache boys learn early in life. It is a half-walk, half-run, and by doing it all day they have been known to travel up to 40 miles without stopping," Mike explained.

"So where do we start?" John asked.

Mike replied, "We'll start where he did, at the rail yards in San Antonio, then travel north. We'll stop at every farm and see if they are missing a horse."

"Sounds like a good plan," John agreed.

They traveled north until dark and stopped at a farm. They asked for and were granted permission to bed down in the barn. They expected to get jerky and biscuits, but the rancher's wife insisted on feeding them beans, cornbread and coffee. They thanked her sincerely and were both soon asleep on a pile of straw.

At daylight the next morning they were in the saddle. That morning they checked three farms with no success.

As they rode up to the fourth farm on their trail they were met by a huge man in bib overalls and pointing a double barrel shotgun in their direction.

"Who are you, and what is your business here?" he demanded to know.

Mike showed his badge and inquired if he was missing any horses.

"Sure am. My best pinto was stolen last night. Two chickens were also taken. Funny thing though. The saddle wasn't taken. I heard a noise and sent the hound outside and we found him this morning with his throat cut," the farmer explained.

John replied, "Just be glad your throat wasn't cut, too. The man responsible for this is Indian Bob. He kills for pleasure. If I were you I'd keep the doors locked for a day or so, to make sure he has left the area."

The two of them continued north and mid-morning they found the ashes of a small fire, surrounded by chicken feathers.

Mike commented, "This is where the bastard ate the chickens."

For two more days they continued riding north, but no sign of Indian Bob. At night they camped with no fire so as not to alert their prey that they were tracking him. The third day as they rode, Mike commented, "I have the uneasy feeling someone is looking at us."

"I feel that way too, as if someone has been watching us all day," John agreed.

That night they built a huge fire, cooked beans with bacon, then arranged two bed rolls next to the fire. Then they slipped into darkness and watched from hiding. Their feelings had been correct. As an hour passed, a shadowy figure emerged from the darkness and shot into both of the fake bed rolls.

Mike yelled at him, "Hold it right there. Drop your gun and put up your hands."

Instead of obeying, the intruder shot at them and attempted to flee into the safety of the darkness. Mike shot once and John three times, and the figure fell. Mike and John both ran into the light of the fire. They both felt sure it was Indian Bob and felt relieved the hunt was over.

Their jubilation was short lived as they got closer and saw that the dead man only had one leg.

"Shit, I thought we had him," John blurted out. "I wonder who this poor bastard was?"

"Judging from the lost leg and the crude crutch he was using, he is probably a Civil War veteran who lost a leg. He probably couldn't make a living so he had to resort to robbing travelers," Mike offered.

John opined, "Well, I don't feel sorry for him. He just tried to kill us by shooting us in our sleep."

"That's true, but I don't want to leave his body out here to feed the coyotes. We'll put him on his horse and take him into the first town we see," Mike said.

The next morning they approached the outskirts of Waco and handed over the body to a deputy sheriff on patrol. Mike explained he was the police chief of Houston, what they were doing, and asked if there had been any sightings of Indian Bob in the area.

After getting a negative response they again headed north aiming for Dallas. After another night of camping out, they were on the outskirts of Dallas.

Both of them were bone-tired, disappointed, disgusted, and dismayed for losing the trail. They stopped at a small settlement and found a livery for their horses, a diner, and a boarding house where they could get a good nights' sleep.

The next morning while having a good breakfast of bacon, eggs, biscuits, and gravy, Mike told John, "You know, fatigue makes cowards of us all. I feel a whole lot better now and I'm ready to take up the trail; you?"

"Me too," John replied. So they retrieved their horses and set out once more, looking for Indian Bob.

They soon were on the same trail heading north. Mike volunteered, "If we don't find him soon, he will be in the Indian Nation, and we may never find him."

After an all-day ride they spotted a dead horse right in the middle of the trail.

John volunteered, "It's a pinto. It could be the one Indian Bob stole."

They dismounted and examined the horse to see if they could determine what killed him. There were no visible signs of injury.

"That Indian bastard probably just rode him to death, with no food and no rest," Mike commented.

They continued riding, but now with more caution, thinking their prey might be near. Not wanting to stop to eat, they ate cold biscuits and beef jerky in the saddle.

Their caution increased as they approached a grove of live oak trees. They kept a close watch ahead and to both sides as they rode.

They were almost into the open at the end of the stand of trees. They had been watching ahead and both sides but they should have been more observant of what was overhead.

After Mike's horse passed, Indian Bob leaped from a tree limb onto the back of John's horse, scalpel in hand. At the instant he landed, John turned to look and the horse bucked, spooked by the sudden additional weight on his back. While struggling to stay on the horse he felt intense pain coming from the right side of his face. Blood was gushing all over his horse, saddle, shirt and jeans. He screamed, "Hey Mike, the son of a bitch cut me!" Then he drew his Colt and shot Indian Bob three times as he attempted to flee into the safety of the trees.

Mike wheeled his horse around and also shot twice. Indian Bob crumpled into a heap.

John dismounted, took a towel from one of his saddle bags, and tried to stop the bleeding. Mike neared on foot and examined the wound, saying, "Oh, hell John, it's a good thing your horse bucked and you turned your head. He was trying to slit your throat. You have a nasty cut on your face, but a few inches lower and you would be dead."

Mike tried to stop the bleeding but could only slow it by holding the towel tightly against the cut.

"John, we'd better get you back to Dallas and find a doctor to sew you up," Mike told him.

"Fine," John said, "but first I have to make sure that bastard is really dead."

John then walked to him and put a .45 slug between Bob's eyes.

Mike tied the body on his horse and rode double with John back down the trail towards Dallas. Mike continued to hold the makeshift bandage to John's face as they rode. The pressure he supplied did slow the blood flow some, but John needed medical attention soon, or he would bleed to death. John was afraid to spur the horse, knowing he would die if his horse gave out on him.

Chapter 8
Recuperating In Dallas

The first house they came to had no lights showing, but Mike went to the door and banged on it until a light went on in the house. Soon a tall man in a night shirt opened the door holding a pistol. Mike explained, "Sorry to bother you, sir, but I'm Mike Ward, Chief of Police in Houston. I have a wounded deputy who has been badly cut and is bleeding profusely. He needs a doctor in a hurry or he will bleed to death."

"Well, you bring him in here and I'll send a man for a doctor. I'm Jeff Combs, the owner of this ranch."

He helped get John into the house and into a bed then said, "You stay here with him until I send someone to fetch the doctor."

Then Jeff went to the bunk house, woke up his foreman, Bill Bonds, and sent him on his fastest horse to bring back Dr. Phillips.

He explained to Mike, "Bill is taking my fastest horse, and Dr. Phillips only lives two miles from here so they will be back soon."

The noise had also awakened Mrs. Combs, who joined them in the guest bedroom where John was in bed. She was introduced as Alice.

Alice asked, "Would you all like some coffee?"

"I sure would, if it isn't too much trouble," Mike replied.

She disappeared into the kitchen.

Jeff then asked Mike, "I noticed a body tied to the other horse; who might that be?"

"That is Indian Bob, a renegade Apache. He killed this boy's parents, raped his sister, then killed two of my best officers when they were bringing him back to Houston from El Paso where he was arrested."

John was drifting in and out of consciousness. They all hoped he would hold on until the doctor arrived.

Alice arrived with a pot of coffee and six cups. Mike eagerly drank the first cup and refilled it immediately. Alice got a clean rag and cleaned the wound on John's face. It seemed like longer but Dr. Phillips arrived in short order.

Dr. Phillips was an elderly man but still hearty enough to make house calls in the middle of the night. He asked everyone but Alice to wait in the parlor while he examined the patient.

The doctor was in with John for the better part of an hour, when he came out of he had a lot of questions he needed answered.

"How did he manage to get a cut that was so precise with no jagged edges?"

"Why was the man so heavily armed?"

"Why was his face cut instead of his throat if his assailant wanted to kill him?"

Mike carefully explained exactly what happened, and the cut was made by a surgeon's scalpel that only missed because the horse reared to get rid of the added weight on his back. He also explained that John was hunting down the men responsible for killing his parents and putting his sister into a comatose state by gang raping and beating her.

Then the doctor explained, "That man has lost a lot of blood and will need to rest for a week before he can ride a horse. I put 12 stitches in his face and closed the wound, but he is going to have a nasty face scar for the rest of his life. I would recommend that tomorrow he has a bath, then gets out of those filthy clothes. Then I will be back in a week and check on him and take out the stitches. And don't try and wake him. He will need to sleep a lot until the effects of the chloroform wear off."

"Thank you, doctor. He has clean clothes in his saddle bags, and I'll get them for him," Mike answered.

After the doctor left, there was still a few hours of darkness left so everyone tried to get a few hours of sleep. Mike curled up on the sofa fully clothed and was soon asleep. Alice was up first cooking bacon, eggs, and biscuits for everyone along with a fresh pot of coffee. John continued to sleep until almost noon. As soon as he heard John awake, Mike went into talk to him.

"How do you feel?" he asked.

"I feel like hell. That chloroform gave me the worst hangover I have ever had," he replied.

John immediately felt the bandage on his face. Then he asked, "Am I going to have a scar?" he asked.

"Probably, but scars just make men interesting to women," Mike answered.

"What do we do now?" John wondered.

"The doctor said you have to take it easy for a week, then he will be back to check on you and take out the stitches," was Mike's answer.

Their conversation was interrupted by Alice bringing breakfast in for John.

"How is my patient?" she asked.

"Well ma'am, I feel hungry and dirty," he answered.

"Well, we can fix the hunger now, and I'll get a bath ready for you later," she responded.

Later that afternoon Mike and John spoke with Alice and Jeff about what would happen now.

Alice started by saying, "You are both welcome to stay here as long as you want to. This is the most excitement we have had here since we ran off the Yankees years ago."

"That is kind of you, but I am going to have to get back to Houston to make sure I still have a job. I'll take John into Dallas with me and find a place to leave him until he is well enough to return to Houston," Mike explained.

Jeff volunteered, "If you can wait until tomorrow morning, I can take you both into town in the wagon, and we'll make John a bed in the back. That would be a lot easier on him, and Dr. Phillips said he shouldn't ride a horse for a few more days."

Mike asked John, "Do you know anyone in Dallas?"

"Well, I don't really know them, but my college girlfriend's parents live there, the Bigelows," John explained.

"Do you mean Clayton Bigelow?" Jeff asked.

"Yes, but why do you ask?" John wondered.

"Well Clayton has two producing wells on the back forty of the ranch; he is really a nice fellow," Jeff responded.

Then Alice interrupted, "And we just love the people who come to empty the oil storage tanks every week. Bob and Nita Ramsey are such lovely and friendly people. Whenever they are short on drivers one or the other of them comes themselves. We enjoy their company so much. Bob is such a good story teller and Nita is so sweet."

"Well, I will ride to Dallas today, look up the Bigelows, and tell them John is here and see what they say. Then I'll send a telegram to my office and tell them I'll be on the next train after I take the stage to San Antonio," Mike explained.

Then John said, "Also please send a telegram to Juan at my ranch, tell him I'm OK and that I'll be back as soon as I can."

Mike said his good-byes, thanks, and rode off to Dallas with Indian Bob's body still tied to John's horse. He intended to turn Bob's body to the Texas Rangers in Dallas so John could collect the reward.

The next morning Clayton and Bambi Bigelow arrived in a two-seat buggy. As they were introduced to John, Bambi said, "You look completely different than the way Lola described."

"Sorry," John said, "But I've been through some tough times the last couple of months, and I'm not the naïve college boy I was a few months ago," John tried to explain.

Then Clayton joined in the conversation, "Chief Ward told us about your recent adventures, and we are here to extend you an invitation to recuperate at our house in Dallas."

"That is very friendly of you, and I accept, but only for a week or so until I get a little stronger," John answered.

Bambi seemed cool to the idea, but showed it only through her body language and attitude.

John went into the house, said good-bye to Jeff and Alice, and then rolled up his two rifles in the clothes Alice had laundered for him. Alone in his bedroom for a minute, he took a $20 gold coin from his money belt and left it on the dresser. John lay down on the rear seat of the buggy as Clayton drove to their home.

John was not surprised to see the mansion the buggy pulled up in front of, as Lola had bragged about her parents' riches. He thought, *This house isn't any larger than the one I lived in when I was young.*

He was still feeling weak as Bambi directed him to his room. As soon as he was alone, he kicked off his boots, took off his gun belt and stretched out on the bed. He quickly fell asleep. He hadn't realized how long he had slept so was surprised when Clayton woke him up telling him it was time for dinner. Before dinner was served, Clayton took him into his office and poured each of them a glass of bourbon.

He diluted it with water and explained the local people called it bourbon and branch, short for bourbon and branch water.

As they enjoyed their drinks, Clayton showed John his elaborate telegraph system, explaining how it was tied to his partner's office, Lola's apartment, Bambi's stock yards in Fort Worth, and the local telegraph office. He could send a wire anywhere. He then told John he had sent several telegrams for Mike. Then they hurriedly gulped down their drinks when Bambi reported dinner was on the table.

John thoroughly enjoyed his roast beef, candied yams, succotash, and dinner rolls. He also had a cup of the best coffee he had ever tasted.

While they ate Clayton entertained everyone with stories of his early days in the oil business. Bambi said very little but John did notice her giving him a scornful look from time to time.

After dinner was finished the two men went to the office for a smoke and a glass of bourbon. Bambi remained behind to help Mrs. Evans, the cook, clean the table. After they were settled into two easy chairs, Clayton asked him, "What are your plans for the future?"

John answered him, "I don't really know, sir. I have been too busy catching the killers of my parents, and the thief who stole the family fortune. I do know that there is a lot of money to be made in bounty hunting, though."

"Yeah, but will you live long enough to spend it?" Clayton offered.

"Yeah, I learned that the hard way," John answered.

"Do you need money that badly?" Clayton asked him.

"No, not really sir. There is still a sizeable estate my parents left. And I do own a 500-acre ranch west of Galveston. I do have my sister to support though. She is still in a constant-care hospital in Houston. She has never recovered from the gang rape and beating the thugs did to her," John explained.

"Yes, Mike told me about that. I'm sorry your family was subjected to that," Clayton said.

"Anyone ever drill for oil in your ranch?" Clayton asked.

"Not that I know of, but I don't think any of the neighbor's ranches have any oil wells on them," John answered.

"Well, it's something to think about for the future," Clayton suggested and they let the matter rest.

After his second glass of brandy, John felt very sleepy, excused himself, and went to bed. He fell asleep right away.

With his belly full of good food and relaxed by two bourbons and a glass of brandy, he slept well. Sometime during the night or early morning he was awakened by sounds of an argument. He stayed awake long enough to overhear Lola and Bambi shouting at each other. He heard Bambi use the words, "Common gunfighter," and "Saddle tramp." He heard Lola answer and say, "OK, then I'll just take him and leave."

If Clayton was involved in this discussion, he said nothing. John did not own a watch and could see nothing but darkness outside, so he went back to sleep. John woke up as soon as he saw a glimpse of daylight. He got up and dressed, just in time. Lola was knocking on his door. He opened the door and told him, "Oh, John, you poor thing. You look a mess. Does that wound hurt?"

As she led him downstairs, Clayton was waiting for them. Bambi was nowhere in sight.

Lola spoke first, "Daddy, we're leaving now. I'll take John to my place until he is well enough to go home. John, go gather up your things. You can rest on the back seat of my buggy and I'll drive."

"Now, Lola, don't go doing something you will be sorry for later," Clayton interrupted.

John, still half asleep, and totally confused, gathered his things and came back down stairs. He said to Clayton, "Sir, I'm sorry I caused this argument. Thank you for your hospitality. I am feeling much better."

Clayton answered, "You are more than welcome, son. We enjoyed having you. I'm sorry you had to witness a family squabble."

There was still no sign of Bambi as John and Lola left in the buggy, with John's horse tied behind the buggy.

After they left there was another argument. This one was between Bambi and Clayton, and was heard only by the cook and the housekeeper.

Clayton spoke first, "Bambi, I am ashamed of the way you treated our guest and of how you spoke to Lola."

Bambi answered, "I don't care what you say. I don't want her to marry the first gold digger that comes along, and especially that boy. He is nothing but a saddle tramp and is not good enough for Lola."

Chapter 9
Recuperating In Austin

"**Y**ou sound exactly like your daddy when he thought I wasn't good enough for you," Clayton answered. "I'm just glad little Sully wasn't here to see how you acted."

"I will not put up with having my daughter marry a dirt-poor bum," Bambi answered.

Then Clayton interjected, "You really don't have your facts straight. That boy is rich, maybe richer than us. He owns a 500-acre cattle ranch, and he and his sister inherited their parents' estate. His father was a very wealthy defense attorney in Houston. He only dresses as he does because he is tracking down the monsters who murdered his parents and turned his sister into a vegetable."

Bambi, still angry, responded, "I don't care how rich he is, I just don't like that little bastard."

Seeing further argument was futile, Clayton retreated to his office and sent a telegraph to Lola. He apologized for her mother's attitude toward John and asked her to apologize to John for him. John and Lola finally arrived in Austin. John was still very tired. He realized he needed more rest before trying to return home. He was glad he had Lola to look after him for a few days. As she helped him into her apartment he asked her to go the next morning and ask Professor Moriarity to visit him. Lola told him, "You look really tired. I'll fix us a bourbon, then scramble us some eggs and make some biscuits. Does that sound good?"

"That sounds more than good. That sounds like a feast to me," John replied. After they finished their bourbon and ate, Lola said, "I know you are too tired to make love, and I'm still too mad at my mother, so we will have to wait for another day. OK?"

"Fine with me," John replied.

The next morning John was rested and Lola had cooled off from her fight, so they started kissing, then touching each other, and soon they were making love. Lola was being very careful about touching his sore cheek, but his other body parts were fair game, and she kissed, touched, and caressed them freely. It had been a long time since he had been this aroused and Lola was enjoying his passion.

This morning had been so enjoyable for both of them they had to summon all of their will power to get out of bed. Lola got up first and made coffee. John followed shortly and they enjoyed their coffee with leftover biscuits with apple butter. Then she kissed John goodbye and left for the university to fetch Professor Moriarity.

She returned before John could finish his fourth cup of coffee. She was accompanied not only by Moriarity, but also a man she introduced as Dr. Paul Hogan, Chief of Surgery at University Hospital.

Lola explained, "Professor Moriarity thought Dr. Hogan should take a look at your wound."

After examining the wound, Dr. Hogan asked, "Who put the stitches in your face?"

John told him, "Some country doctor near Dallas. Why, is anything wrong with them?"

"Oh no, he did an excellent job, but I'm afraid you have an infection in the wound. What kind of knife did the cutter use?"

"A surgical scalpel," John answered.

"Well, I'm going to take the stitches out and put some medicine in the wound. Can you stand a little pain?"

"I think so, Doctor. Go ahead," John told him.

John winced a few times causing Lola to rush to him and hold his hand. Soon all the stitches were removed and Dr. Hogan added a green salve to the open wound.

"What is that stuff?" John asked.

"It's a salve made from tree moss. The Indians have been using it for years. It will take away the infection. I'll leave the jar with you so Lola can apply some more for a few more mornings," the doctor answered.

"Will I have a scar?" John asked.

"I'm afraid you will have a hell of a scar, but don't worry about that. Girls like scars. They think it makes a man look interesting," Dr. Hogan said, as he winked at Lola.

"Thank you, Dr. Hogan," John told him.

Then Moriarity asked, "John, what is it you want to see me about?"

"I'm happy to tell you I found Samuels and recovered most of the bearer bonds, so if you can I would like you to look at them, calculate their worth, and give me a bill for your services. I hate owing money," John said.

"If you give me a week, I can be gone for a few days," the professor replied.

"How about Lola? Can she be off for a few days too?" John wondered.

"Sure can. She is so far ahead of the rest of the class, she could miss a week and not fall far behind."

John spent the next week resting; being waited on by Lola, and making love almost every night. Lola went to class every day so she could take the following week off. John checked his face in the mirror every morning and saw the wound was almost healed. The doctor had been right about the scar. He had a scar six inches long just along his right cheek at the jaw bone. He hoped his appearance would not be objectionable to Lola.

Before they left John had Lola use her telegraph to send a wire to Juan at the ranch telling him they would arrive Saturday afternoon.

Chapter 10
Safe at the Ranch

The three of them left in Lola's buggy, Lola seated in the middle with John on one side and Moriarity on the other. John kept his Winchester and Sharps at his feet. No matter how hard the local sheriff's departments and Texas Rangers patrolled, a lot of robbers still preyed on stage coaches and private buggies.

As they pulled into the ranch Juan greeted them, along with Lisa and Maria. Lisa ran to the buggy saying, "John, what happened to your face?"

"Let's go to the house and I'll tell you all about it, after I have a drink," John answered her.

Lola turned to John and said, "Oh John, this place is so beautiful. Does it all belong to you?"

"Yeah, me and my sister," John answered.

Then Maria interrupted, "John, speaking of Sarah, Lisa and I were in Houston last week and we went to St. Agnes to check on her. I'm afraid there has been no change at all but Sister Ruth asked about you."

"I only wish I could make Sarah understand I killed the last of the bastards that put her in that state," John said.

Lola asked, "Who is Sister Ruth?"

"She is a nun, and the prettiest nun I have ever seen," John answered noting a slight tone of jealousy in her question.

The next week passed quickly. John rested, enjoying the attention he required from Lola, Lisa, and Maria. Moriarity spent his time examining the recovered bearer bonds and calculating a bill to present to John.

By the end of the week his wound had healed enough that Lola removed the bandages. She silently gasped to herself as she noticed the scar which now dominated his facial features. The scar was six inches long and ran directly along his right cheek bone. She hoped it would be less noticeable when it was completely healed.

On Saturday morning, John was sorry to say good-bye to Lola and Moriarity as they both had to return to school. He sat and watched them until they were completely out of sight. He secretly wished he was going with them to spend more time with Lola. Lisa had been watching him and said to him, "You miss her already, don't you?"

John nodded yes.

Lisa continued, "Well John, she is a nice girl, so sweet, and she is in love with you."

"I hope so, because I think I love her too," John answered.

Chapter 11
Back Home in Houston

The following day John saddled his horse, packed up the rest of his father's suits from the ranch house, and headed for Houston. Upon arrival he first went to St. Agnes Hospital to see Sarah. Sister Ruth met him walking down the corridor, hugged him, then looked at his scar as she asked him, "How did you get hurt?"

"Well, Sister, a murderous Indian tried to slit my throat, but God protected me," John answered.

"Why, John, did you just say God protected you? You told me you were an agnostic."

"I was, but something has been looking after me lately, and it has to be God," John told her.

"I knew you would see the light sooner or later, and thank God you have. God bless and keep you," Sister Ruth said.

Then Sister Ruth escorted him to Sarah's room. John thought to himself, *How thin and frail she is.*

Then he pulled up a chair to Sarah's bed, sat, and said to her, all the while knowing she could not hear a word of what he was saying:

"Hello, sweet sister Sarah. I just wanted you to know I have taken care of the four monsters that did this to you and our parents. I also caught up with Samuels who robbed us, and he is in jail. I just wanted you to know."

Then he kissed her on the forehead and left to check in with Chief Ward. Mike greeted him warmly, saying, "That is some memento on your face. Seriously, it looks a lot better than I thought it would."

"What's the deal with Samuels?" John wanted to know.

"He is safely in jail and has signed a confession. He will be sentenced next month and probably will spend a lot of years in Huntsville Prison," Mike assured him.

Having made his rounds John headed to the Wedgewood, called for a bath, a glass of bourbon, and bed.

That night he slept long and hard but was awakened at dawn by someone loudly knocking on his door. He answered it to find a messenger from the Western Union.

Chapter 12
Trouble in Dallas

"I have an urgent telegraph for Mr. John King. Are you Mr. King?"
He grumpily answered, "Yeah, kid, I am. Hand me the telegram.
He ripped open the envelope, handed the messenger a nickel, and read
the wire. It was from Lola.

> *Urgent. Sully has been kidnapped. Need you in Dallas*
> *right away. Please take early stage today and I'll meet you*
> *tomorrow when stage arrives. Love you. Lola.*

John dressed hurriedly, threw some clothes into a carpet bag, and
had the livery attendant drive him to the stage depot. There were coffee
and rolls at the depot so he ate hurriedly before boarding the stage. His
carpet bag was stowed on the top, but he took his Winchester inside
with him.

Lola met him and rushed him to her parents' house. Waiting there
was Clayton, Bambi, and a man unknown to him.

The stranger was introduced as Pete Bowers, who ran the stockyards
for Bambi.

Clayton hastened to hand a letter to John. It read:

> *Deer rich oil man. We got your kid. If'n you want him*
> *back it'll cost you $10,000 in coins. No paper back money.*
> *No police. You have three days to git the coins, or we send*
> *you one of his ears or fingers. When you got the money take*
> *down the Texas flag in ur yard and we give you way to*
> *bring money.*

"Where did you get this?" John asked.

"It was shoved under our front door day before yesterday," Clayton answered.

"Got the coins?" John asked.

"Yes, I have them, and I have been waiting for you to get here before I take down the flag," Clayton explained.

John noticed Bambi was crying loudly. "We'll go take down the flag, and we'll just have to wait for another letter," John instructed him.

Lola asked him, "Are you hungry?"

"I sure as hell am. I haven't eaten since yesterday morning," he replied.

Hearing that, Bambi quit crying long enough to go have the cook fix John some lunch.

As he ate, Lola said, "Thank you for coming. We didn't know who else to turn to."

"Well you've got that cowboy in there. What does he do besides run the stockyards for your mother?" John said.

"That's all I know, except he is supposed to be good with a pistol," Lola replied.

"Oh, huh," John said with his mouth full of ham and cheese sandwich.

With the flag taken down, they only had to wait for another letter.

As they waited, Clayton offered all of them a glass of bourbon and branch.

John answered, "Make mine a double."

Pete replied, "No thanks, I don't drink."

John thought to himself, *How admirable.*

Lola joined Clayton and John in having a drink, as Pete went into the kitchen to console Bambi.

John asked Clayton, "Do you have any enemies that would do this to you?"

"Not that I know of," Clayton replied.

It must have been while they were eating a great dinner of barbecued ribs, beans, and potato salad that another letter had been shoved under the door. After they finished eating, Lola found it and read it aloud.

OK rich man u got the gold. Ur boy is Ok but don't be if u try anything cute have ur wife or daughter--no men--bring

it and go down Nacogdoches Road or the boy dies. Do it by
noon tomorrow.

Then Pete spoke up, "Maybe you could get some other woman to go. I don't want Lola or Mrs. Bigelow risking their lives."

John answered him, "It's too damned bad what you want. Lola will go, and I will be there to protect her."

"But how? They said no men," Pete asked.

John ignored him and asked Clayton, "Do you have a closed coach?"

"No but my neighbor does, and four white horses to pull it," Clayton answered.

"Well, when it gets a little darker go ask him if you can use it tomorrow. And see if he has a coachman's uniform you can borrow," John instructed.

In about an hour Clayton returned with a coachman's uniform and permission to use the coach.

"Good. Now where is the gold?" John asked.

Clayton pointed to six bags in the corner, saying, "It is very heavy. I had to go to two banks to get that much."

"Well, let's divide it up into at least twelve sacks. Any sacks will do, even pillow cases if necessary. The more sacks the longer it will take them to load it," John recommended.

"What do you plan to do?" Clayton asked.

"Well, if Lola is willing, I will dress up like a coachman and drive her and the gold down Nacogdoches Road and try to get your boy back. Now we'd better all try and get some sleep," John explained.

Lola agreed to take the gold, and John told her, "You are a brave lady."

Clayton and Bambi retired to their room.

Lola announced, "Pete, I have put some blankets and a pillow on the sofa; you can sleep there. John you come with me; I have made you a pallet."

John followed her down the hall and asked, "Where is my pallet?"

"I am your pallet. You can sleep on me."

And she took his hand and led him into her bedroom. They instantly started making love, then went to sleep holding each other, knowing they had a big day tomorrow.

Lola was still asleep when John dressed in the coachman's uniform and went to the kitchen table. He joined Pete for coffee.

Pete asked, "What is my part in your plan for today?"

"Well, I notice you wear a tied-down holster. Are you any good with that pistol?" John inquired.

People tell me I am the fastest draw they have ever seen," came the answer.

"Have you ever killed anyone?"

"No. And I hope I never have to," Pete replied.

"Well Pete, let me give you a piece of advice. Don't ever draw your gun unless you plan on using it. Don't shoot unless you plan on killing someone. A wounded man can kill you just like a healthy one can. Make sure they are dead," John advised him.

"Thanks. I'll remember that," Pete replied.

"Now about today, I would like you to stay here and guard the Bigelows," John told him. "You married?" John asked.

"No, but I have a girl picked out I would like to marry. But there is a problem. You know I am an Aggie from Texas A & M, and she is a tea sipper from the University of Texas. And the two schools are arch rivals," Pete said.

John thought to himself, *Uh oh, he is talking about Lola. This guy isn't happy just running the stockyards, he wants to own them.*

Soon the whole household was gathered at the table for breakfast.

Clayton jokingly told John, "You look funny in that coachman's suit."

"The suit must belong to a very big man. The pants are so large I was able to put them on over my pistol belt. The coat is so large it will easily hide my shoulder holster holding the Remington," John told him.

After everyone finished breakfast, they all went outside to load the gold into the carriage.

John advised, "They are probably watching us right now, so let's take our time loading and make sure they see us loading all of the bags."

John had previously stored his Winchester under the driver's seat, so he opened the door for Lola to enter the coach. In doing so, he handed her his Derringer, telling her, "Keep that out of sight. Only use it if I am dead or wounded."

She answered, "Don't talk like that."

John closed the carriage door, climbed onto the driver's seat, and set out for Nacogdoches Road. He quietly asked God to look after the two of them and get Sully back alive.

They had been traveling for almost an hour when a masked rider, with pistol drawn, blocked their path.

"HALT. Hey driver, who the hell are you?"

"I'm Jonah, the coachman, and I'm driving Miss Bigelow," he lied.

"Well, get down from there and open the door," the masked man demanded.

John obeyed, and out of the corner of his eye he could see another man hiding in the bushes.

When the door was opened, the masked man looked inside the carriage and told Lola, "Open one of those bags."

He dug his hand in the bag and pulled out a handful of $20 gold coins.

Lola then spoke up, "OK, there's your money, now give me my brother and we'll be on our way."

"Not so fast. What is that driver doing here? I said no men," the masked man asked.

"He is our coachman. I don't know how to handle four horses. Now please give me my brother, take your gold and let us go." The man examined three more bags then yelled, "OK, Donny, back that wagon down here and help me load this gold."

As the wagon neared, John saw Sully bound and gagged in the rear of the wagon. He furtively removed the pistol and shot the driver twice. The other masked man drew his pistol and got off a shot in John's direction before John killed him with three shots. As John started to relax a little, another man galloped toward them.

John was surprised, not counting on there being three of them. He calmly climbed into the driver's seat, retrieved his Winchester, took careful aim and blew the rider out of the saddle. Then John, for insurance, put one more bullet into the heads of all three men.

Then he took out his pocket knife and cut the ropes from Sully's hands and feet and removed the gag from his mouth. Lola rushed to help Sully out of the wagon. He was trembling, partly from fear, but also from the poor circulation from being bound for so long.

"Oh Sully, I'm so glad you are OK," she said.

"I'm OK now, thanks to that man. But who is he?" Sully said.

Then Lola hugged John and said, "Thank you. You were wonderful."

"Are you OK, Sully?" John asked.

"I'm fine, thanks to you," he replied.

"Good," John said, "Then help me load these pieces of garbage into the wagon."

The gold safely in the carriage, Sully driving the wagon, John driving the coach, and the third man's horse tied to the wagon, the strange looking caravan made their way back into Dallas.

As they reached the Bigelow's house, Clayton, Bambi, and Pete were all waiting for them.

Bambi and Clayton rushed to Sully, hugging and kissing him.

Sully said, "Mommy and Daddy, I was so afraid. That man saved my life."

Bambi and Clayton rushed to the carriage, hugged and kissed Lola to determine if she too was safe. Then they all gathered around John. Clayton warmly shook his hand saying, "Thank you."

Then Bambi hugged him and kissed him on the mouth. She said, "I will never be able to repay you."

Lola laughingly said, "Careful mother, he is mine." Everyone laughed except Pete.

Sully spoke up, "I am starved. Could I have something to eat? It has been days since they fed me."

Pete approached John, "How did you do it?" he asked.

"Well, I just shot them. The third man was a surprise, but no match for my Winchester," John calmly told him.

"Weren't you afraid to go up against three of them?" Pete asked.

"Hell yes, I was afraid, but not so scared I was going to just stand there and be killed," John answered.

Then Clayton volunteered, "Let's all go in, and I'll open a bottle of champagne to celebrate."

John replied, "Make mine bourbon and a double, then I have to do something to get rid of those dead bodies."

"Let's have a drink first, then I'll go with you to the sheriff's office. Sheriff O'Leary is a friend of mine so there won't be any questions about why they were killed," Clayton explained.

"Sounds good, but let me get out of this monkey suit. I'm sure glad I don't have to make a living as a coachman," John told him.

Chapter 13
Visiting Sheriff O'Leary

When they arrived at the office of Sheriff Bob O'Leary, they found the office manned by a deputy. Clayton told him who he was, and the deputy left at once to get Sheriff O'Leary from his home. In short order, Sheriff O'Leary came in, shook hands with Clayton, and was introduced to John.

"Oh yes, that bounty hunter from Houston. I have been looking for you. We still owe you $2500 for bringing in Indian Bob."

John look surprised, as he had forgotten all about it.

Then O'Leary continued, "Well, Clayton I recall 25 years ago, when you and Billy Smith brought me dead bodies. Who have you killed now?"

"I didn't kill anyone, Bob. These three dead men kidnapped Sully, and John here was bold enough to get him back for me. He had to kill these three to get my son back."

O'Leary ordered the deputy to get some help and bring the bodies into the office. After checking the faces of all three men and comparing them to wanted posters, O'Leary pronounced, "These are the three Skaggs brothers, Ronny, Donny and Pooge. We have been chasing them for some time. They have held up two banks here in town and robbed two stage coaches, but I didn't know they graduated into kidnapping."

Clayton responded, "Well, they have. They took Sully and wanted $10,000 for him."

"How did you kill them, son?" O'Leary asked.

"Well sir, I dressed up like a coachman, drove Lola with twelve bags of gold coins, and shot two of them when they were moving the gold to their wagon. I killed the third one with my Winchester when he galloped up firing wildly at us," John told him.

"That probably was Pooge. He was always a little short on brains, and he would do anything his brothers told him to," O'Leary responded.

Then Clayton said, "Will you take care of the paperwork for us, Bob?"

"I can do that Clay; I'll bring you a copy of the report this afternoon, and another county check for John here, later this afternoon."

"Good, come by and have a drink with us," Clayton offered.

"You can count on that. See you this afternoon."

As promised, Sheriff O'Leary showed up at the Bigelow home. He did enjoy the bourbon and branch, and handed John two checks. He explained, "Here is one check for $2,500 for Indian Bob and $1500 for the Skaggs boys, $500 apiece."

"Thank you, Sheriff," John responded.

Pete had already left for Fort Worth, but the others celebrated late into the evening.

After a few drinks, Bambi told John, "I will never be able to thank you enough. Come see us anytime."

"Thank you ma'am," John responded.

Clayton quietly told John, "I won't insult you by offering you money, but if there is anything I can do for you. Anything at all."

John responded, "Thanks. I will ask something of you, but not right now. I'll ask it in a year or two."

"Just let me know," Clayton said.

The next morning John and Lola left for Austin, Lola to resume school and John to wait for the stage to San Antonio, then the train to Houston.

Chapter 14
Back Home in Houston

Upon arrival in Houston, he hired a driver to take him to the Wedgewood. Before he went to his room, he went into the stable to check on his horse, Diablo. He found him well cared for.

The girls behind the desk greeted him warmly as he picked up his key.

John thought to himself, *It is good to be here, but I miss Lola already.*

His plan was to rest the next day then go to visit Sarah, and check in with his friend Chief Mike Ward.

John never considered his visits to Sarah a waste of time. He knew there was a little chance she could understand what he said to her, but he felt compelled to tell her about his activities. He related the kidnapping and recovery. And his new relationship with God. Then he kissed her forehead and left her room. These visits were hard for him, but he felt obligated to see her.

As he left the room, he met Sister Ruth, who took his hand and welcomed him warmly.

"Oh, John, I am so concerned about Sarah. She is not eating, and she resists us when we try to force feed her. I fear she is tired of living in her condition and wants to die," she said her eyes welling with tears.

"Oh, no," John responded.

"I'm afraid she is in God's hands now, so we will pray for her," Sister Ruth said.

"Sister Ruth, I am happy to tell you, I now have a relationship with God. He has protected me and I have thanked Him for it. So I will also pray to God for Sarah," John reported.

She responded, "God bless you, John. I knew that would happen sooner or later, and I am glad it is sooner."

Asking Sister Ruth to keep him advised, he left for the police station.

After shaking hands, John followed Mike Ward into his office.

John came directly to the point, "Mike, I am concerned about Sarah. She refuses to eat and acts as if she wants to die."

Mike answered, "I'm so sorry John, but I think I might respond the same way if I was in the same situation. What can I do to help?"

"Well, I had planned on moving to the ranch, but now I hate to do that under the circumstances," John explained.

"Well it has been my experience that people never die when we expect them to. I have an idea, though. If you want to go ahead and move down there I will check on her every day, and if it happens I'll dispatch someone to fetch you right away."

"That's a great idea, Mike. Thank you. You are a real friend," John told him.

With his mind more at ease, John rode to the Wedgewood, gathered up a few clothes and rode to the ranch. When he arrived he met with Lisa, Maria, and Juan. He explained the situation with Sarah to them, and his plans to spend most of his time at the ranch. Then he sent a letter to Lola informing her and telling her of Sarah's latest prognosis. He planned to give the letter to the mail rider so it would get mailed earlier.

For the next few weeks John busied himself learning more about the day-by-day ranch routine.

Chapter 15
Sarah Dies

One day a rider arrived with the news John had been dreading. Sarah had died. John had tears in his eyes as he thanked the rider, a police officer, and invited him to stay for lunch.

After lunch, John saddled Diablo and rode back to Houston with the police officer.

His first stop was at St. Agnes. He met with Sister Ruth, who hugged him and told him, "Oh John, I know you are sad, but you should also be glad her ordeal is over and she now has a better life in heaven."

"Thank you, Sister. I know she is in a far better place, and much happier," John replied.

"John, I will be happy to assist you any way I can. If you are interested, we have a small chapel here and our chaplain, Father Declan Carroll, will be happy to say a requiem mass for her," Sister Ruth offered.

"Thank you, Sister. Can we have the funeral a week from today? That will give me time to invite friends who live out of town," John said.

"Of course we can do that. With your permission I will make the arrangements and let you know when it is all arranged," Sister Ruth told him.

John then went to talk to Chief Ward and tell him the news.

Mike gave John his condolences and offered to help any way he could.

Then John headed for the telegraph officer and sent a wire to Lola, knowing she could inform her parents. He then spent the night at the Wedgewood before leaving the next morning for the ranch.

During his ride to the ranch he, of course, felt sorrow but also a great deal of relief. He knew he would miss the young girl he knew and loved. He would not miss the poor creature who was bed-bound.

Sarah's funeral was crowded. The small chapel in the hospital was filled to overflowing. Lola; her parents, Clayton and Bambi; Professor Moriarity; Mike Ward and his wife, Carol; Juan, Lisa, and Maria from the ranch; and Sister Ruth, who sat by John for moral support, were all in attendance.

John had never attended a Catholic funeral before, and told Sister Ruth later how much he appreciated the serenity of the service.

After Sarah was laid to rest in the cemetery adjoining the hospital, everyone but Sister Ruth adjourned to the Wedgewood for an informal wake. John had made arrangements to use the ballroom for the party. He also made reservations for a guest room for the Bigelows. He hoped Lola would stay with him, which she did.

He knew Moriarity would stay with his lady friend, and Juan, Lisa and Maria would leave early to return to the ranch. Clayton asked John to meet him for coffee early the next morning, and he was waiting when he arrived at the coffee shop at that time,

"Good morning, John. I hope it is not too soon after the funeral to talk business," Clayton greeted him.

"Oh no, actually poor Sarah left us all some time ago," John replied.

"Well, I wondered if you had thought any more about us drilling some exploratory oil wells on your ranch," Clayton said.

John replied between sips of coffee, "Yes, Juan and I have discussed it, and we agree the best place to start would be on the south pasture. The soil there is so salty we have a hard time getting a good crop of hay there anyway."

"That could be a good sign. There may be a good salt dome under there that just might have oil beneath it," Clayton replied.

"Well then, just go ahead and start drilling there when you are ready," John agreed.

Clayton offered his hand and John shook it. Clayton said, "It's a deal. Now let's talk about the details. I'll pay you a quarter override, and for a signing bonus I'll pay for a telegraph line to be laid between your ranch and Galveston. That way you can communicate with Lola or me, or anyone in the country who has access to a telegraph. Lola is an excellent telegrapher, and I'm sure she could teach you in short order."

"Sounds fine with me," John agreed.

Clayton answered him, "Great, I'll have the papers drawn up and bring them to you as soon as I can. But now I remember you have a favor to ask me. Ready to ask me yet?"

John replied, "Yes, sir, I think I am. Lola graduates next year, and with yours and Bambi's permission, I would like to ask her to marry me."

"I hoped that is the favor you would ask, and so did Lola and Bambi. We would be delighted to have you for a son-in-law," Clayton answered.

"Good, I'll go buy a ring today and ask her. But please don't tell her yet. I want it to be a surprise," John answered.

It wasn't long before Lola and Bambi joined them and they ate breakfast together.

Bambi asked, "Have you men been talking business?"

"We sure have. John agreed to let us drill some exploration wells, and I have agreed to string a telegraph line from Galveston to the ranch. And Lola, I hope you don't mind, but I volunteered you to teach him to use the key. Is that alright?" Clayton informed them.

With a huge smile, Lola said, "That's great. I more than agree. It will be a pleasure."

John also smiled and winked at her.

After they all finished breakfast, John excused himself saying he had some errands to run. He left the Bigelows to discuss the morning's happenings amongst themselves.

John rode straight to Gildemeister's Jewelry Store. He knew the owners from the days his mother purchased jewelry from them. He selected a three-carat diamond, and while he waited they set it in a wide gold band. He also purchased a wide band plain gold ring to match.

Paying them with cash from his money belt, he rode back to the Wedgewood to ask Lola to marry him.

Finding the Bigelows gathered in their room with Lola, John sat down to talk to them, the ring secreted in his pocket.

Clayton spoke first, "John, Bambi and I are taking tomorrow morning's stage direct to Dallas, but Lola is waiting and will take the train day after tomorrow, with Moriarity, to San Antonio, then the stage to Austin. Is that OK with you?"

"Good with me," John replied.

John and Lola borrowed a buggy from the livery and drove Clayton and Bambi to the stage station.

Clayton told him, "Thanks for everything, and I'll be back in a week or so with some papers for you to sign."

Bambi told him, "Good luck, John," and winked at him.

John thought to himself, *Boy that lady's attitude towards me sure has changed since I first met her.*

That evening John drove to the Stockyards Steak house for dinner. He had never been there. But Mike Ward told him they had the best steaks in town. After two bourbons each, John proposed to Lola. She accepted and he put the huge diamond on her finger. She gave him a very lusty kiss, telling him, "That will have to hold you until we get home, and then I will really thank you."

John flashed a broad smile. After a delicious dinner they drove back to the Wedgewood, and went to the bedroom, holding hands.

True to her word, Lola treated John to some fantastic sex. He was unaware she knew some of the tricks she showed him.

They went to sleep early, partly because they were worn out from the sex, but also knowing they had to rise early to get Lola on the morning train to San Antonio to connect with the stage to Austin.

Moriarity met them at the depot, and they left.

John waved good-bye to them, went to the Wedgewood, traded the buggy for Diablo, and rode to the ranch.

Chapter 16
Preparing for the
Ranch to Change

After enjoying lunch with Juan, Maria, and Lisa, John explained to them the changes that would take place.

1. In several weeks, oil drilling would begin in the south pasture.
2. A telegraph line would be laid between the ranch and Galveston.
3. He would be starting construction on a new wing to the ranch house where he and Lola would live after they were married next year.

The first two changes drew very few gasps of surprise, but the third one caught all three of them by surprise. John was overwhelmed by their handshakes, hugs, and kisses of congratulations.

John spent the afternoon going through the safe and the files maintained by his meticulous father. He found the deed and the original plans for the house showing the builder, Jose Garcia and Sons, in Galveston. Then next morning after a breakfast of bacon, eggs, and biscuits with gravy he took the plans, saddled Diablo, and rode to Galveston. He found the Garcia Builders were not only still in business but had prospered. He met with them and laid out his ideas for the new wing to the house. He said he wanted three bedrooms, an office, a living area, and a guest room. Jose studied the plans for a few minutes then suggested adding two new wings, one on either side of the house. He could add three bedrooms and an office with a family side, and then put the guest wing on the other side of the house. John liked the idea and Jose told him he would draw up the plans and deliver them to him at the ranch the following week. He wanted Lola to see them before they started building. The following week John was surprised to see Clayton arrive. He was even more surprised to see Lola and Sully with him.

After kissing John, Lola ran to the house to show her ring to Juan, Maria, and Lisa. She got the same hugs, kisses, and handshakes that John received the week before.

Then Clayton took John aside to tell him, "I have another favor to ask you. Sully is a typical spoiled rich kid. He doesn't want to study or apply himself, and only wants to drink and party."

John thought, *That sounds like me before I had all this responsibility laid on me.*

But he asked, "What can I do to help?"

"I wondered if you could give him a job here at the ranch, and work his ass off. No special treatment, just treat him like you would any other hand," Clayton told him.

"Well, I'll have to talk to Juan, but I think we can work out something," John told him.

Clayton continued, "Lola is on spring break and brought a practice telegraph key with her, so you should be ready to send by the time the wire is installed, week after next. Now I have some papers for you to sign."

John told him, "Sounds good. I'll get Lola to San Antonio to catch the stage to Austin when she is ready."

The next morning soon after Clayton left in the buggy. Jose Garcia arrived with the plans for the house. Lola loved the plans, as did John. After agreeing on a price, Jose left, promising to start on the remodeling in one week. Lola and John began his lessons with the telegraphy key. After two readings John's amazing memory had completely memorized the Morse code, so Lola began teaching him how to use the key.

Within a few hours he had mastered what took other people two weeks to accomplish. Another week went by and John hated to take Lola to the stage because he knew it would be weeks until he saw her again. He was glad to leave the busy goings on at the ranch. The house was in shambles from the construction, Western Union people were installing poles and wires, a drilling rig was busy drilling exploratory holes in the south pasture, and Sully was busy digging fence post holes for a fence to separate the south pasture from the other three pastures.

As they rode to San Antonio in the buggy, John told Lola, "That place is like a Chinese fire drill. I'm glad to be away from there for a while."

Lola answered, "I know it is hectic now. but it will soon calm down, and you will wish I was back with you."

"You're right. I will miss you. I'll be lonesome, alone in that big bed without you."

Lola then, very unexpectedly changed the subject asking, "John, have you thought about where we should be married?"

"I couldn't care less, just as long as we get married," John answered.

"Well, I have been thinking about it a lot. Mother wants me to have a big church wedding, but I just want a small ceremony with only a few friends and family there," Lola reported.

"Whatever you want is fine with me," John agreed.

"I would like for us to be married in that little chapel at St. Agnes. I just loved that little place, and that Father Carroll was so nice. Next time you go to Houston, ask Father Carroll if he will marry us, please."

He promised to do so.

After a tearful good-bye, Lola left on the stage and John went to the Menger for a good night's rest before leaving for the ranch the following morning. The Menger was his favorite hotel and the bar there was his favorite bar. He loved the dark paneling and the bar where a huge hand-carved back bar dominated the room. Little did he realize that years later Teddy Roosevelt would also visit this bar and recruit his "Rough Riders" here.

After a good night's sleep he rode back to the ranch, missing Lola already.

In three months the house renovations were completed, the telegraph wire had been strung, and Sully had developed into a hard-bodied, muscular young man, who no longer had a bad attitude.

Pleased with the progress, John sat down at the telegraph key and sent the following wire to Lola:

Bedlam over with here. House completed, telegraph installed, Sully has new body and attitude. Only thing missing is you. What about graduation? Love you. John.

Within an hour John had an answer to his wire:

Glad for you and Sully too. Graduation is two weeks from Saturday.

Mom was not happy about wedding arrangements but will go along with me. Did you talk to Father Carroll? I love you too. Lola.

With all of the confusion at the ranch John had not visited Houston but would go there tomorrow to see Father Carroll.

The next morning John saddled Diablo and rode to Houston. It felt good being on Diablo; it had been a while since he had ridden him.

On arrival he went directly to St. Agnes, said "Hello" to Sister Ruth, then went to visit with Father Carroll. When he asked if he would marry him and Lola, he got this response in Father Carroll's best Irish brogue, "Faith and begorrah, that would be my pleasure to do that. It seems all I do is say funeral masses, and a wedding will be such a great pleasure for me."

John felt relieved and left for a men's clothing store. He bought a brown suit and a blue suit. He made sure the suit coats were loose on him to disguise shoulder holsters. He was abandoning bounty hunting, but with all of the enemies he made, he was not about to go around unarmed.

After spending the night at the Wedgewood, he left early for the ranch. Upon arrival there, he sent the following wire to Lola:

Saw Father Carroll today. He will be delighted to marry us. See you soon at your graduation. I'll bring Sully. Love you. John.

Chapter 17
Lola's Graduation

John and Sully arrived at Lola's already crowded apartment on Friday afternoon. Clayton and Bambi were there, as were Clayton's partner, Billy Smith, and his wife Betsy. Bambi instantly pushed to Sully telling him, "Oh, my God, I almost didn't recognize you. Your pale face is all tanned, and your skinny little arms are bulging with muscles. What happened to you?"

"John and Juan worked me so hard! At first I hated them, but now I realize they were helping me grow up. I will never be able to thank them enough," Sully answered.

John kissed Lola, then made his way to the kitchen where there was a make-shift bar. Soon Professor Moriarity arrived to join in the festivities.

Later in the evening, the party stated breaking up and everyone was leaving for the hotel rooms they had rented.

Lola took John's hand and whispered to him, "You stay right here. We're going to have a private celebration later."

John smiled and squeezed her hand, and they did celebrate that night, enjoying sex as if it had been a long time, which by their standards, it had been.

The ceremony next morning was a short one, with only eleven graduates in the class. Lola graduated Summa Com Laude, which made her parents proud. Several Dallas and Houston law firms had agents at the ceremony offering jobs to the graduates. Lola received several job offers, but her standard response was, "Thank you, but I'm going into private practice with him," pointing at John.

After a quick lunch, John helped load Lola's things into a wagon. She would be moving back to Dallas until the wedding.

John watched as the wagon and buggy left for Dallas, then he headed back to the ranch. It was a long lonely trip.

As he entered the gate and started up the road to the ranch house, Juan ran toward him saying, "John, I have good news. The first well came in and is already producing oil. I hope you don't mind but I let the driller use your telegraph key to notify Clayton."

John answered, "Sure, it's OK, Juan. I'm glad you did. By the way, that kid Sully told his mom and dad what a good job you did with making a man out of him."

"I'm glad he feels like that. He wasn't a bad kid, just spoiled rotten," Juan said.

When he walked into the house he was greeted by Lisa and Maria, who also were excited about the good news. Then as he sat at the kitchen table with Lisa and Maria, he told them about the wedding plans. He invited them to the wedding and handed each of them a $10 gold piece telling them, "Use this to get yourselves a new dress for the wedding."

"*Gracias, gracias,*" they told him.

Chapter 18
The Wedding

The time flew by until it was time to prepare for his wedding. One of the reasons time passed so quickly was due to the excitement of the second well blowing in.

The small chapel at St. Agnes was filled to capacity. On the bride's side of the aisle sat Clayton and Bambi; Billy and Betsy Smith and their son, William; two friends of Lola's from school, Donna and Gloria; Sully, and Professor Moriarity.

On the groom's side sat Lisa and Maria, Juan Ortiz, and Sister Ruth. Mike Ward was to be best man and his wife, Carol, would be matron of honor for Lola. John had met Carol before, but he had never seen her looking so lovely. Her 4'11" frame nicely supported her school-girl figure, which remained unchanged despite giving birth to two daughters. Her blonde hair outlined her remarkably young-looking face. John thought to himself, *Just look at her. She looks young enough to be the bride.*

Her petite stature was a sharp contrast to Mike's 6'4" stocky build, but they made a beautiful couple.

Father Carroll drew a chuckle from the group as he announced, "This will be such a joy for me to be able to unite these two beautiful people. Weddings are one of the few pleasures this old man has left in life."

The mass was short but very well done. After the ceremony, everyone (except Sister Ruth) adjourned to the Houston Petroleum Club. Clayton had arranged for use of the club through the Petroleum Club in Dallas where he was a member. Father Carroll went with them, telling Clayton, "I'd be honored to join you. I have an ulcer and I'm not supposed to drink, but being an Irishman, I will have a little Irish whiskey in a glass of milk."

The brunch they were served was unlike anything John had ever seen: eggs benedict, bacon quiche, French toast, a fruit bowl, and always full glasses of champagne or cups of coffee.

After everyone had eaten their fill, the waiter emerged from the kitchen with a huge five-tiered wedding cake.

Everyone eagerly washed down the cake with champagne or coffee, regardless of how much they had eaten.

John and Lola had decided against taking a traditional honeymoon. They planned to spend the night at the Wedgewood, where John had also arranged guest rooms for the out-of-town guests. Then the next day they would go to the ranch and get settled in.

John opened the door to his room, picked up Lola, carried her into the room, kicked the door shut behind them, and deposited her, gently, on the bed. There, on the nightstand was a magnum of champagne with a card saying, "Congratulations!" courtesy of the Wedgewood.

"Now we can do it legally," he announced.

"Not just yet, sweet heart. It's not like we have never done it before, and we have the rest of our lives to do it legally. First I want you to open your wedding present. I can't wait to see if you like it," Lola told him.

She handed John a beautifully wrapped package with a card that read, "To my wonderful husband, my best friend, and the light of my life."

Saying, "Thank you, sweetheart," he kissed her. Then he ripped open the package and exposed a beautiful oak case, about 24 inches square. "What in the world is this?" he asked.

"Open it, open it," Lola excitedly told him.

John opened the hinged lid exposing a tray with lots of compartments. One compartment held three pairs of dice, carved from ivory; one compartment held three decks of playing cards; three compartments held poker chips of different colors, denoting values. The center compartment contained a miniature roulette wheel. All of the cards and chips were monogrammed with a large capital "T."

"This is absolutely beautiful," John said.

"Remove the tray," Lola instructed him.

John obeyed, removing the top tray. It then exposed a lower tray that held a silver-plated ivory handled, Colt pocket revolver; an ivory handled bowie knife; a set of brass knuckles; and an ivory-handled double barrel, silver-plated Remington Derringer.

John whistled then told Lola, "I think I know what it is. I have heard of them, but have never seen one."

"What do you think it is?" Lola asked.

"I think it is a traveling gambler's kit. Where in the world did you ever find it?" John wondered.

"Daddy found it for me. He bought it from a man who said it was made for a famous gambler named Ben Thompson. I hope you like it," Lola said.

"Like it? I love it, and I love you for getting it for me. But I left your wedding present at the ranch. I'll give it to you tomorrow," John told her.

The night was spent making serious love to each other.

The next morning, as John had arranged, they had a late breakfast delivered to the room. By eating late, they hoped the majority of out-of-town guests would have left for home.

That turned out to be the case because when they left for their ranch, everyone else was gone.

They arrived at the ranch and saw the presents Juan and the girls had brought with them. Lola also noticed a large present in the corner, covered with a sheet. John told her to remove the sheet, and she saw a beautiful western saddle, with her initials on each side, "LK," in silver *conchos*. She looked a little bit disappointed, so he led her to the stable and showed her the rest of her present. It was a buckskin- colored mare. She gave a scream of delight and hugged the mare.

The next morning, after Lola went room to room inspecting the new addition to the house, the two of them rode off together. Lola wanted to see the ranch, and John wanted to see the new well that had just come in. That ride was the beginning of many morning rides they would take together as they settled into a new life on the ranch.

Chapter 19
Visitors at the Ranch

From time to time welcome visitors arrived to visit John and Lola. One Sunday morning Chief Ward, Carol, and their two daughters arrived. They were interested in showing their daughters the ranch. Their older daughter, Elizabeth, was crazy about horses. The younger one, Kimberley (Kimmie), was more interested in seeing the ranch house. Maria took Kimberley on a tour of the house. Lisa busied herself in the kitchen preparing lunch for all of them. Lola took Elizabeth to the barn, saddled her mare for her, and watched her ride away as John, Mike, and Carol sat on the porch and chatted as they enjoyed their coffee.

John said, "Mike, it is good to see you and Carol and to meet the girls. Thank you for bringing them."

Mike responded, "It is good to see you too, John, especially when we don't have to ride so many miles in the saddle. And fight our way out of some place."

Elizabeth was more interested in riding the buckskin than she was in eating, so she continued riding while the rest of them enjoyed their lunch of ham sandwiches, baked beans, and potato salad. The Wards left for Houston mid-afternoon so as to get home before nightfall. It had been a pleasant day for all of them, and they promised to return soon. John put his arm around Lola, and they watched as their buggy disappeared from view. John commented, "I owe Mike a lot, including my life."

Lola answered, "Then I owe him a lot too, because I can't imagine a life without you," and she kissed him hard and lustily.

The next month passed quickly. Maria helped Lisa with the cooking for John and Lola, Juan, and the twelve ranch hands. Maria and Lisa went to the market every Friday and brought home a wagon load of food and supplies. They made Mexican food several times a week, and that was fine with John and Lola. They loved the spicy taste. John and Lola were still very much in love and proved it to each other by making love several times a week.

It was a Sunday morning and John and Lola were sitting in the porch swing finishing their morning coffee, when they watched as a wagon made its way toward the ranch, on the road from Corpus Christi. As the wagon neared Juan rushed to meet it. It was Tomas and Rosita, who had come to visit from Monterrey. Juan shouted, *"Buenos dias,"* and escorted them to the porch. Juan introduced them to Lola, then kisses and hugs were exchanged. Hearing the commotion, Maria and Lisa joined the festivities. Tomas apologized for the surprise visit and explained they had mailed a letter to them two weeks ago. He said he was not surprised that it had not arrived yet. "That is just the way my country's mail works. *"Todo es manana."*

John told them, "I am so glad that you accepted my offer, and I hope we can show you the same kindness you extended to Juan and me when we visited you."

Rosita said, "That was our pleasure having you, and I hope we can all visit each other more often. Juan is our only living relative, and we miss our family."

Lola then offered, "Well, I hope you will consider all of us your family. We certainly would welcome you into our circle of family."

Rosita answered, "Well, consider it done. We will all be just one happy family."

After lunch Juan saddled three horses and took Tomas and Rosita on a tour of the ranch. Tomas was interested in seeing the producing oil well as he had never seen one before.

He commented, "Those oil pumps look like pictures I have seen of dinosaurs."

John and Lola were waiting on the porch for Juan and their guests when they returned from the ranch tour. Maria and Lisa were also waiting for them with a pitcher of margaritas. Even before the pitcher was emptied, they all sat down for a dinner of tamales, rice, beans, and tortillas.

Rosita and Lola helped clear the table while Lisa served dinner to the ranch hands in the bunk house. John and Tomas adjourned to the porch to enjoy coffee and a cigar.

John asked, "What ever happened to Carmen?"

"Oh, she is fine. She wanted to come with us, but she couldn't miss school. She is going to college. She wants to be a school teacher, and I think she will be a good one," Tomas reported.

"I agree. That poor girl has had enough adversity to last a lifetime," John said.

Maria had prepared the guest room for them and all were tired and ready for an early bed time.

After an early breakfast the next morning, Lisa made them a basket of sandwiches to eat on the train, and Rosita and Tomas said their good-byes and rode off for Corpus Christi to board the train for Monterrey. Lola had expected the next visitors they would entertain would be her parents, but so far they had not shown up. A wire from Bambi explained that Clayton was working seven days a week training Sully to take over more responsibility in the oil business.

It was a Wednesday about noon when a buggy was spotted heading towards the ranch on the road from Houston. Juan spotted the buggy first and ran to the house to get John, who was busy working on the payroll.

"Hey, boss, do you know those folks?" Juan asked.

John looked through the window, and without answering he strapped on his Colt Peacemaker, and walked to the porch. Seeing this, Juan took a Winchester rifle from the gun case and followed John to the porch. It was Willie Washington and Linda.

Seeing Juan holding the rifle, Willie shouted, "Don't shoot, Mistah! We ain't got no guns, and we mean nobody no harm. This is a friendly visit."

John answered, "You are both welcome. Come on up here."

Linda explained, "We stopped in Houston and Chief Ward told us how to find you. We both just came here to thank you for what you did for Willie."

John asked, "And what would that be? All I did was turn him over to the sheriff in Nacogdoches."

"Oh no—you did a lot more than that! You turned over the reward, and the sheriff was able to hire Attorney Calhoun for him. Calhoun convinced the judge to only sentence him to 60 days in jail. Then the sheriff gave him the money that was left over, and we put that with some money I had saved, and we bought the diner together. Willy is the cook and I am the waitress, and we are making money," Linda told him.

John answered, "Well, I am sure happy for you two. If it hadn't been for Willie, I wouldn't have been able to catch up with the killers of my parents."

Willie chimed in, "Thank you, Mr. King. Thank you for everything, suh."

John said, "I am just glad it all worked out the way it did. Thanks for taking the time and effort to come here to tell me."

All of that said, John watched as Willie and Linda rode off in the buggy, waving good-bye.

When John went to the table for dinner that evening, he was still wearing the gun belt.

Lola, unaware of the visitors, asked, "Why are you wearing that gun belt?"

"Don't worry, sweetheart. I am taking it off, and hopefully I will never have to put it on again," John answered.

Lightning Source UK Ltd.
Milton Keynes UK
UKOW042355081112

201882UK00001B/120/P